ONE MORE NIGHT

Lauren Blakely

Book # 3 in the New York Times
Bestselling Seductive Nights Series

ALSO BY LAUREN BLAKELY

The Caught Up in Love Series

(Each book in this series follows a different couple so each book can be read separately, or enjoyed as a series since characters crossover)

Caught Up in Her (A short prequel novella to
   Caught Up in Us)
Caught Up In Us
Pretending He's Mine
Trophy Husband
Playing With Her Heart
Stars In Their Eyes (releases August 2014)

Far Too Tempting

A standalone romance about a rock star and critic, this book also ties into Stars in Their Eyes.

The No Regrets Series
(These books should be read in order)

The Thrill of It
The Start of Us
Every Second With You

The Seductive Nights Series

(The first four books follow Julia and Clay and should be read in order)

First Night
Night After Night
After This Night
One More Night
Nights With Him (Fall 2014 - a standalone novel about
   Michelle Milo and her lover Jack Sullivan)
Untitled #6 (Brent's book, January 2015)

The Fighting Fire Series

Burn For Me

Stay tuned for more sexy firefighters, including Megan and Becker's story coming soon!

ABOUT

One More Night
Book #3 in the New York Times
Bestselling Seductive Nights Series

Your presence is requested for another installment in the tale of Julia and Clay, two red-hot lovers. Come inside their world of passion and suspense once more for a deliciously erotic and heart-poundingly dangerous story of pearls, handcuffs, thieves, mobsters, poker and pleasure in the city of sin...

Happy endings don't come easily. They're hard-won and Clay Nichols is going to have to keep earning his...

Now living together in New York with her debt safely paid off, sexy bartender Julia Bell and hot-as-hell entertainment lawyer Clay thought their future was clear sailing.

But life doesn't work that way and the fiery lovers run into a slew of new challenges as Clay tries to put a ring on it. Trouble looms in every corner—trouble from clients, trouble with timing, and, most of all, trouble from her past returns on their trip to Vegas. A dangerous man who knows much more about Julia than he should surfaces in Sin City where they're supposed to be enjoying a weekend getaway. Following her in the casino, watching her every move at the pool, targeting her as she plays poker.

Too bad Clay is called away repeatedly, leaving Julia alone in a sprawling hotel full of dark corners, back rooms, and unsavory characters. Can Clay save her from danger one more time, and then finally get down on one knee? Or will he be too late for the woman he adores?

Read on in ONE MORE NIGHT, a novel in the New York Times Bestselling Seductive Nights series packed with more sex, more dirty talk and more danger. And per your request, the recipe for Julia's award-winning cocktail, the Purple Snow Globe, has finally been revealed in this ebook!

DEAR READERS

This book exists because of you.

When I finished writing AFTER THIS NIGHT I thought their story was done. *Mostly.* As you know, Julia and Clay have a happy ending in that novel, but the possibilities for what's next in their future are left open. Within hours of that book releasing, I started receiving requests from readers for *more*. So very many of you emailed me, messaged me, posted on my wall and mentioned in reviews that you wanted more Julia and Clay, and that you wanted to know what happened when they went to Vegas. So here you go! But get ready. This isn't just a mushy love-fest. It's not all hot sex and declarations of love, though of course there is plenty of action between the sheets. But Clay and Julia exist on these pages because of the trouble they attract in their lives. Because of conflicts. Because of challenges. They have a new story to tell because they face more danger in their lives. So kick back, grab a Purple Snow Globe, and get ready for a bumpy, naughty, dirty, thrilling ride.

DEDICATION

The book is dedicated to Cynthia and Malinda for that night in New Orleans when they helped me find the right next story for Clay and Julia; to Jen, who guided me around certain bends in the road during the writing, especially those involving handcuffs, music and locations, and to my fabulous husband Jeff, who shows me the way out of every plot corner I very nearly paint myself into.

CHAPTER ONE

Thursday, 9:03 a.m., New York

from: cnichols@gmail.com
to: purplesnowglobe@gmail.com
date: August 14, 9:03 AM
subject: You, naked and sound asleep in bed this
morning . . .

You have no idea how hard it was for me not to wake
you up before I left for work and do bad things to you.

from: purplesnowglobe@gmail.com
to: cnichols@gmail.com
date: August 14, 11:18 AM
subject: Just waking up now . . .

I'm a little confused. Did you just say you declined to
do bad things to me? I can't think of a single reason
why you would do that.

from: cnichols@gmail.com
to: purplesnowglobe@gmail.com
date: August 14, 11:22 AM
subject: Get your rest while you can . . .

Every now and then I'm a gentleman in the bedroom, and you needed your sleep. Especially with the things I plan to do to you this weekend. I won't be a gentleman then.

from: purplesnowglobe@gmail.com
to: cnichols@gmail.com
date: August 14, 11:43 AM
subject: Then I won't be a lady . . .

Not just bad things, I hope. But very bad things? We are going to the city of sin, after all. I expect no stone unturned in your sinful pursuits.

from: cnichols@gmail.com
to: purplesnowglobe@gmail.com
date: August 14, 11:55 AM
subject: All stones overturned and then some . . .

I have so many sinful things planned for you that I'd be stopped at the border. That is, if Vegas had a border.

from: purplesnowglobe@gmail.com
to: cnichols@gmail.com
date: August 14, 12:07 PM
subject: Frisk me, please

Are you going to tell me anything about this weekend? Will I, for instance, be handcuffed?

from: cnichols@gmail.com
to: purplesnowglobe@gmail.com
date: August 14, 12:16 PM
subject: You look good with your wrists bound.

You won't get a word out of me on that front. All I have to say is this: Just. You. Wait.

CHAPTER TWO

Friday, 8:36 a.m., New York

Her hair a wild tumble and her eyes still hazy from what Clay had done to her, Julia sat up in the leather seat of the town car and glanced out the tinted window, catching a glimpse of the houses rolling by. Some red brick, a few yellow clapboard, all with freshly-mown lawns and crisp hedges. Pulling her gaze away from the glass, she tugged her skirt back down to her knees, then flashed a woozy thank-you-for-the-fantastic-*O* smile at her man.

He winked as he adjusted his tie—his lucky purple tie. Earlier this morning, he'd been wearing a sun-yellow silk tie that she'd bought for him at Barney's a few weeks ago for no reason except that she knew it would look good on him. Indeed, the tie accentuated his power attorney style perfectly when he wore it to an important meeting the next day, and it had looked particularly fetching on her later that night when he'd twined it around her wrists then lifted her onto the kitchen counter and had her as an appetizer before they both enjoyed dinner.

But even though she had fond memories of the yellow tie, she'd insisted he wear the purple one today. It was a trip to Vegas after all, and they'd be gambling for fun, so they needed Lady Luck on their side. Whatever good fortune this tie had brought him, she wanted it traveling all the way to the city she hadn't visited in a long while. The place she'd despised on principle for the last few years, but was ready to fall in love with again on this trip.

"Now, that's a way to start a vacation," she said, snuggling next to her handsome man who'd just pleasured her. That was one of his favorite things to do, and he'd brought her many *O*s in many town cars over the last few months, starting with that first weekend she'd visited him in New York.

He'd treated her quite well in moving vehicles. Come to think of it, he'd treated her well every-fucking-where and back.

"There's more where that came from," he said, as he wrapped an arm around her, pulling her in close.

"I never expect anything less than a regular supply of your talented mouth," she said, running her palm along his square jawline, locking her gaze with his deep brown eyes that knew her so well. She threaded her fingers through his thick hair, simply because she could, simply because it was damn near impossible to keep her hands off him. She moved in for a kiss, but something in her peripheral vision nagged at her. Those houses beyond the window.

Houses? That's when it hit her. There were no houses on the way to the airport. There were no manicured lawns and pretty porches on the path they usually took. It was highway all the way, but she'd been too preoccupied moaning, writhing and rocking her hips against his face the last several minutes to notice.

She dropped her hand from his hair and narrowed her eyes. "This isn't the route to Newark," she said, her voice a bit panicked.

He tilted his head and scratched his jaw. "Hmmm. It's not?"

She tapped the window. "Look, Clay," she said. "This isn't the way we usually go. I think your driver is going the wrong way. We need to let him know."

"You better tell him then."

She hit the button for the partition. The glass that separated their sprawling leather pleasure den from the driver lowered with a soft swishing sound.

"Hey there," she said in a chipper tone.

"Yes, ma'am. What can I do for you?"

"I think we might have taken a wrong turn. I'm not sure this is the way to Newark, and we have to catch our plane in an hour."

"We'll make the flight no problem, ma'am."

"Oh. So you're going to turn around now?" she asked, leaning closer to the front. The corner of the driver's lips twitched, as if he were suppressing the start of an errant smirk.

"There's a back route I know to the airport, ma'am. It cuts through this town. We'll be there soon," he said, his hands on the wheel, his eyes on the road, the little sliver of a smile threatening his lips.

"If you say so," she said, playfully. "How long till we reach the airport?"

"About five minutes."

"Thank you so much. And by the way, thanks for making this such a smooth ride," she said, then tossed a naughty look at Clay, who knew exactly why she'd been barely aware of her surroundings when he'd buried his face between her legs a few minutes ago, then sent her soaring and screaming. She returned to her seat, and whispered to Clay, "That's odd, don't you think? I've never heard of a secret back route to Newark. You'd think everyone would know about it. Or that it's the sort of in-tel that would get shared among friends. Do you think we'll catch that United flight? The next one was booked, and I have that meeting with Farrell Spirits at two, Vegas time."

He reached for her hand, threading his fingers through hers, squeezing tight. "There's not a chance in hell we aren't making it to Vegas on time. I promise you that. You will make your meeting, and we might even be early. When I checked the flights this morning, the weather was smooth sailing all through the friendly skies."

She arched an eyebrow, not quite sure where his cocky confidence about air travel was coming from, but then not caring when she realized there was a small window of opportunity to perform her favorite job. Stabbing the partition button once more, she sealed them off from the driver, and wedged herself next to her sexy man, dropping her hand on his crotch, delighted to discover he was still completely aroused.

"You are still hard from what you did to me," she said in a purr.

"Gorgeous, I'm hard nearly all the time being around you."

"Then I need to do something about it, because we have five minutes and this driver gives one hell of a smooth ride."

"Then let's get those lips of yours wrapped around me and see what kind of ride you can give me," he said, the gravel of his voice sending a flurry of tingles down her spine.

"You know I love a challenge, Clay. And I'm going to give it to you good right now."

"You always do. But I'm not easy. I don't know if you can pull this off in five minutes," he said, deliberately taunting her.

She wagged a finger at him, then unzipped his dark blue jeans in one quick move, tugging his briefs down too. "I know exactly how to lick, suck and touch your cock for a two-minute, a five-minute and a ten-minute blow job," she said, then dropped her mouth onto his erection, taking him all the way in in one smooth, quick move.

He groaned instantly. "Maybe," he said, as if he didn't believe her. "But which one is this going to be?"

She licked him back up to his head, then rubbed him against her lips, because she knew that drove him wild. Seeing his cock being caressed and loved by her mouth was his undoing. His eyes darkened, and he shut them briefly, his head falling back against the leather seat as he speared her hair with his strong fingers. "Get those lips back where they belong. All the way around me."

"It's going to be the two-minute treatment then," she said, blowing a stream of air against him, and he opened his eyes to hitch in a breath. "Say you want it fast. Admit

I can make you come in two minutes," she said, rubbing his throbbing erection across her lips once more to show him she knew the path to his pleasure.

"Do it," he growled.

That was all she needed to reacquaint his cock with the back of her throat, wrapping her lips tight around the base, and sucking hard. She cupped his balls, rolling them against her fingers, and that drew out a long, deep groan. She smiled to herself at his reactions, loving that she could do this to him. She continued on her quest, sucking hard, licking teasingly, and delighting in every second of it as his groans grew louder and his fingers gripped her tighter. She finished him off quickly, savoring the taste of him in her mouth and the sound of his grunts in her ears.

When she returned to her seat as he zipped his jeans, she nearly shot out of the moonroof as the signs for Teterboro Airport loomed closer.

"This is definitely not Newark," she said, her voice practically a shout. "Where are you taking me?"

"Welcome to the executive airport, gorgeous. We'll be flying in a private jet to Vegas."

CHAPTER THREE

Friday, 8:58 a.m., New York

"Ladies first," Clay said, gesturing to the steps that unfolded from the gleaming silver Cessna that looked like a bullet. She squeezed his arm, then walked up the steps. *No, that was wrong*, he corrected himself. She *strutted*, wiggling her sexy ass for him, happily heading into the jet.

Keeping her busy on the ride over had been the best distraction—in and of itself—and because it preserved the sheer surprise that he'd wanted to elicit from his woman. The jet was one part of the weekend he'd mapped out for Julia in Vegas. Every detail was planned to a T; every gift arranged in advance. He wanted to shower her with luxuries, capping them all off tomorrow with the one he was most eager to give her—a three-carat emerald-cut diamond ring as he asked her to be Mrs. Clay Nichols forever and ever. The ring was safely in Sin City already; he'd had it shipped from Tiffany's, and sourced from a diamond mine in Canada, one of many that operated by socially responsible guidelines in the diamond business. His brother, Brent, had the ring under lock and key at his place in Vegas. Clay had contemplated having the ring shipped to the home he and Julia shared in the West Village, but when she'd playfully confessed one evening last month while lounging on their balcony, drinking scotch and looking at the stars, that she'd been the kid who peeked at her Christmas presents early, he knew it was safest to keep the ring far away from her prying eyes.

"McKenna almost ratted me out one year. She found me re-taping a Christmas package early one morning when I was ten, I think. My face turned bright red, but then I told her our cat was playing with an ornament, and had knocked a few presents around, so the tape must have come off."

He'd laughed at her cover-up. "And she believed that far-fetched, multi-layered fib?"

Julia shook her head, a self-deprecating grin curving her lips. "Nope. So I tried another tactic. I gave her my most prized possession in exchange for her silence—my scrapbook of all these fabulous Jordan Catalano snapshots from *My So-Called Life*," she'd said, and he'd smiled at the mention of the TV show she and her sister had been huge fans of when they were growing up. That was something else he and Julia had in common; not that show, but an affection for movies and TV as entertainment and as touch-points for special moments in life.

"You are deviously clever, and I also want to thank you for the advance warning that I should never leave any Christmas gifts for you under the tree until Christmas morning when Santa arrives."

She'd pretended to pout. "No fair."

"So fair," he'd countered, as his mind whirred through the best options for keeping a ring far, far away from those exploring eyes and fingers. When he'd told her at her bar the other night that he'd planned to take her to Vegas for the weekend, she'd blatantly stated that she hoped he might get down on one knee, so he certainly wasn't trying to catch her off-guard with his proposal. They were open with each other about their desire to be married someday soon. But the details? The where, when, and how of it? That's what he could have fun with, moving puzzle pieces around, keeping her on her toes and hopefully finding a way to surprise the woman he loved, adored and cherished.

Starting with this jet. *Mission accomplished on the first surprise.*

"All this for a Friday meeting in Vegas?" she asked, as she drank in the posh interior. Her meeting with Farrell Spirits, the global beverage giant that manufactured Julia's very special, very secret drink, had proved to be fortuitous timing. He'd already booked the trip when a few days ago one of the marketing executives at Farrell had asked her to meet in Vegas, where the company's U.S. marketing operations were headquartered. Farrell wanted to expand Julia's role from a behind-the-scenes mixer of its wildly popular new drink into a sort of spokeswoman for the Purple Snow Globe she'd invented. Once that serendipitous meeting was set, he had the perfect alibi to make this weekend seem like it was simply a combo business-and-pleasure getaway, not a well-planned and orchestrated opportunity to pop the question.

"You've got to be able to fly with the high rollers now that you're becoming one," he told her, sliding his palm over her ass, cupping her cheek through her skirt as they stood in the galley. "Think of it as your corporate jet for the day, courtesy of the Pinkertons."

The Pinkertons, a duo of British film-producing brothers, had offered him the use of the jet for the weekend; their way of saying thank you for all the points he had won them in the deal they'd just signed with a studio for their newest movie.

As Julia stepped into the lush inside of the jet, he watched her take it all in. Her green eyes were wide and bright, practically inhaling the surroundings as she stopped in her tracks. Her jaw dropped and she gawked.

That made his heart pound against his chest. He loved her unfettered reactions. She didn't hold back. She didn't pretend. She let her emotions show through, and she was clearly in awe right now, which was exactly how he'd wanted her to feel. Pride suffused him as he catalogued her response. She wasn't a woman who needed a private jet; she'd happily fly commercial, but she sure as hell was a woman who appreciated gifts, and did he ever love giving things to her.

She launched herself into his arms and rained kisses on his cheek, jaw, and neck. "I am so glad you are making them boatloads of money, because this jet rocks. You are getting ten thousand blow jobs for this one, mister," she said.

"That's a lot. You better get started."

"You're ready again so soon?"

He pretended to look at his watch. "Soon? If memory serves the last one was twenty minutes ago. That seems like a lifetime in between to me."

She let go of him and strolled further inside, running her hand along the soft, leather seats. In a warm shade of beige, they were spacious, complete with footrests and full reclining ability. The Cessna Citation X had nine seats, and he'd never been so grateful for an empty flight than he was today. At the back of the plane, a metallic bar boasted sleek bottles of vodka, scotch and other liquors, sturdy tumblers, and a bowl of fresh, ripe strawberries, courtesy of his clients.

The Pinkertons liked him.

A lot.

"This climbs to 51,000 feet, and the weather forecast indicates smooth sailing across the skies," a friendly voice informed them. They turned around to find the pilot had joined them. Dressed in a dark suit and a pilot's cap, the silvery-haired veteran of the skies quickly introduced himself.

"Greg Barton. I spent twenty years in the air force before moving to the private sector," he said as he shook hands with Julia, then Clay. "I promise you'll enjoy this flight so much, you may never want to get off the plane." He returned to the cockpit to begin his preparations.

Julia picked up on his comment, and ran her fingers down the buttons on Clay's shirt. "I suspect this will indeed be my favorite flight ever, though I kinda doubt it'll be because of the smooth sailing."

He arched an eyebrow. "Maybe I just want to nap rather than join the mile-high club."

"We'll just have to see about that," she said, then walked across the plush carpeting to the bar, reached for a strawberry and popped a particularly red and juicy-looking one into her mouth, her lush lips closing around it. He couldn't wait for the plane to take off.

CHAPTER FOUR

Friday, 10:03 a.m., flying above Ohio

Somewhere around one thousand feet in the air, Julia fell asleep. It was pretty much instant. She settled into her cushy seat, leaned into the comfy headrest, intending to close her eyes only briefly, and then crashed. She'd been working hard at her bar, and working late, so he figured she needed the extra shut-eye, not to mention a weekend off her feet. Her hours at Speakeasy, the bar she was part-owner of in Manhattan, had been long and late into the night, and as a bartender she was always standing. He hoped she'd be able to relax some this weekend after her meeting, and maybe spend time at the spa or pool at the new Allegro Hotel where they'd be staying on the Strip.

With her quietly snoozing, he took his laptop from his bag, and flipped it open. He had a few contracts he could get a jump-start on as well as some emails to power through. The plane had Wi-Fi, so he logged into his email. He'd planned to take the weekend off, but he wasn't much of a napper so he could use this time to get ahead on next week's workload. His clients kept him busy, and he liked it that way.

He fired off answers to several notes, one from his counterpart at a studio, another from Flynn at his firm, and one more from Liam, an actor he represented who owned Speakeasy. After a successful Broadway run in *The Usual Suspects*, Liam had landed the plum leading role in a new heist flick set to start shooting soon. That movie was one of the reasons Clay had booked a penthouse suite for the weekend at the Allegro, the backdrop for a few key scenes in the upcoming movie.

As he typed, a silent alarm popped up on the top of his browser. When he saw it was from an Etsy seller, a quick burst of hope rushed through him. He'd been hunting for something perfect for Julia, a one-of-a-kind item to include in the parade of gifts this weekend. A Purple Snow Globe necklace: it would be the finishing touch, if the seller could pull it off. He'd found a similar item—a shiny emerald-green martini glass pendant, but he'd needed it in purple, and had asked the seller for a custom order. The seller was talented, but not terribly speedy, so he wasn't sure if it would be done in time. She couldn't find the right clasp—she only had a long, T-bar clasp. He'd told her *fine*. Whatever, he'd take a different clasp.

He simply wanted the pendant on the chain. He rubbed his palms together and clicked on the note. Ah, there it was. Ready. He replied with a confirmation, adding that he'd like to pay for a same-day delivery service to the Allegro Hotel.

A new note landed in his inbox from Gino Rizzo, an executive at Comedy Nation, who put the *p* in *prick* when it came to negotiations. Clay had been brokering a deal for a producer client of a new late-night show, and Gino had railroaded every point. He read the note, his chest tightening and his fists clenching with every word. Damn bastard was threatening to walk if Clay didn't take care of the final clause today.

He shoved a hand roughly through his hair, and slammed his laptop shut. If he left it open, he'd send a nasty email. Instead, he rose and paced up and down the short aisle of the jet. He ran through options as he wore a tread on the plane's carpeting. The silent ride and the smooth hum of the engines cleared his head, becoming the soundtrack he needed to figure out what to do next. His client, a one-time sports announcer, needed this deal. Desperately. He'd struggled mightily to get this far in his career, and Clay couldn't leave him hanging. The guy had a wife and four kids, one of whom had needed multiple surgeries to correct a birth defect. The gig with Comedy

Nation was the first nibble his client had had in a year, and he needed that deal.

Fuck.

That meant one thing.

The key to negotiating power was being the one willing to leave everything on the table. In this case, Clay wasn't the one willing to walk away. He hated not being in that position. But if his client wouldn't walk away, he couldn't, so he'd have to walk—or fly, rather—to the other party.

Parking himself back in the seat, he opened his laptop, and banged out a reply.

Fifteen minutes later, Julia stirred. He turned off his computer once more, stood up to root around for his bag under the seat and locate one of her wrapped gifts, then returned to the seat next to her as her eyes fluttered open. "Hey handsome," she murmured.

"Hey gorgeous."

"What have you been up to?"

"Working."

"Always working," she said, shaking her head

"I could say the same for you," he said, planting a gentle kiss on her forehead, the gift box tucked by the side of his leg. He swallowed, wishing he didn't have to say the next thing. "Hey, I hate to do this, but Rizzo at Comedy

Nation is playing hardball, and I have to get things ironed out."

"He's such an ass," she said, her voice coated in irritation. "I wish you could punch that guy."

He laughed, loving her put-up-your-dukes nature. "Trust me, I would like to land one on him."

"So you need to go to L.A. instead of Vegas?"

He nodded, the corner of his lips curving into a frown. "For a couple of hours. I don't think I'm going to be able to join you at the Farrell meeting. But if you absolutely want me there, I'll find another time to see Rizzo."

"No. I know Grant needs this deal," she said insistently, referring to Clay's client. The fact that she knew the names of his clients and that she cared about his business had always touched him. What he did for a living mattered deeply to him; he liked that the details mattered to her too. "It's absolutely fine. I am a big girl and can handle my meeting."

"I know you can. I just wanted to make sure."

"And then after my meeting, I plan to have a date with a lounge chair and a Pina Colada poolside at the Allegro until you return. I can just kick back and work on my non-tan," she said, gesturing to her creamy, fair skin that she always covered in sunscreen. Then she placed her hands together in a prayer, as if making an oath. "But in the meantime, I promise not to agree to anything or to sign a thing without my lawyer looking at it," she said, giving him a sexy little wink.

An appreciative moan escaped his throat. "Mmm. I have taught you well the perks of being with a contract man."

"Want to play lawyer and naughty client?" she said suggestively, running her hand along his thigh. "Oh, Mr. Lawyer, I'm thinking of signing on the dotted line when you're not around."

"I'll put you over my lap and spank you."

"That'll only make me want to go wild with blue ink," she said, playing the part well. She quickly changed her tune as she placed a palm on his chest and raised an eyebrow. "You sure you're not sneaking off to Los Angeles to get me a ring?"

He laughed once more. She'd been trying to get it out of him since the night he told her he'd wanted to take her to Vegas for the weekend. Even with her business meeting, she was hunting for clues of a proposal. Only his brother knew he planned to ask her to marry him this weekend. "I'm not going to Los Angeles to get a ring, but even if I were I would never tell you," he said.

"You do realize that gives absolutely nothing away?"

He nodded, tapping her forehead lightly, then running his finger down to her nose. "I know," he said, then nibbled on the end of her nose.

"Well, enough about rings. What's in that box there you're hiding by your leg?"

"You saw it?"

"My gift-spotting skills know no bounds."

He handed her the turquoise-wrapped box with a white bow on it. She eyed the bow. "In case you want to tie me up on the plane, looks like we already have something to use."

His dick twitched against the denim of his jeans. She was always on the same wavelength as he was. "I may need to tie up your hands as a reminder to bring your poker face to the meeting today."

She gave him a sharp-eyed stare. "Do not ever doubt my poker face. It is masterful," she said, as she tugged one end of the ribbon, letting the white satiny bow fall across the shiny wrapping paper. Ripping off the paper, she popped open the top of the box, and there it was. That glow in her eyes. The absolute joy in receiving gifts. She was a delight to give presents to because she never faked her appreciation. Reaching inside the box, she wrapped her fingers around the necklace then gently lifted the long strand of pearls. "Oh my God, they're stunning. They're so fucking gorgeous."

She draped the pearls over her hand, the long strands like waterfalls of smooth, rounded beads. She gazed at them like they were precious, a fitting response, since they were. "They're real," she said, with wonder in her voice as she looked up at him.

He nodded. "I would never give you something fake."

"I've never had pearls before. I've never thought of myself as a pearl person."

"Then let me show you how I want you to wear them, so you can see how absolutely fucking sexy a pearl person can be," he said, standing up and making his way to his suitcase. He opened one of the zipper compartments where he'd tucked a dress for her, and brought it over. "Another gift. Put this on."

"Now?"

He nodded. "Yes. Model it for me."

"As you wish," she said, standing up and glancing once at the cockpit. "What about the pilot?"

"I told him we'd be making full use of the plane and he said he'd have his eyes on the sky the whole time."

"Then keep your eyes on me," she said, looping the strand around her neck, then stripping off her skirt, letting it pool at her feet, her gaze locked on him the whole time. He watched her, growing harder with each layer she removed—now her shirt, then her lacy bra. He reclined the spacious leather seat, taking in the show, savoring every second of her undressing. She stood before him in only her underwear, a small bit of sheer white covering her pussy, the evidence of her arousal already starting to show as he caught a quick glimpse between her legs.

"There's no need for the panties. Get rid of them now, Julia," he told her in a rough voice.

She nodded, and stepped out of the panties.

Taking the silky dress from his hands, she tugged it on, and he shuddered, jealous of the fabric that now hugged her naked curves. She turned around, but kept looking at him, watching as he caught sight of the backless dress for the first time.

He drew a sharp breath, letting it fill his chest as the view of her bare skin fueled his desire. "Come here. I need to adjust those pearls," he said, and she kneeled in front of him. In one quick move, he shifted the strand from her front, dangling between her breasts, to her back, so the pearls were a choker on her neck. "Now sit on my lap, so I can admire you," he said, and she rose, then positioned her sweet little ass on his thighs. He smoothed his hands over the soft skin of her back, his cock stiffening as she hitched in a breath at his touch. Unable to resist her breasts, he looped his hands around to cup them through the fabric, kneading and stroking until her nipples quickly turned to hard diamond points. She gasped, and arched her back, pressing her breasts further into his hands as if she needed the pressure, craved the touch. He played with her breasts until she was nearly panting, then returned his hands to her gorgeous back, and the trail of pearls that led down her spine. "I can't decide if I want you to wear these while I fuck you or if I want to play with them while I'm fucking you," he mused, as he fingered the pearls.

"How would you play with them?" she asked, and her voice sounded hot, wanton.

"Let's find out," he said, grasping her hips and lifting her off him. "Unzip my jeans, woman. I can't fuck you with my clothes on."

That wicked grin spread across her face with his words. She skimmed his pants down to his knees, unbuttoned his shirt and spread her palms over his chest as she stood between his legs. Electricity shot through him; she alone could do this to him. She was the only one who had the control panel to his body, who knew which dials to turn and how far. She pressed his nipples between each thumb and forefinger, squeezing hard. He nearly growled in response, his eyes momentarily drifting shut.

"I'm so tempted to sign things without you around," she teased, as she licked his chest, returning to their role-playing.

He stopped her hands, moving them behind her back. "I see you're already trying to get in trouble with your attorney. I warned you what would happen."

She shivered. "I'm ready to take my spanking."

"But this time it's going to be different, Julia. I'm not going to use my hand," he said, as he removed her necklace. Gripping the necklace carefully in his hand, he left a small loop hanging down, then quickly swatted her backside with the pearls.

"Oh!" she gasped.

"I'm not sure I was clear the first time. You might need to hear it again."

"Oh yes. I think I might, to fully understand the *impact* of what you're saying," she said.

"Good. Because I need you to listen to me." He lightly spanked her marvelous bottom with the pearls and she bit her lip, an absolutely delicious image of her trying to rein in the pleasure that was likely roaring through her body. If the way she felt matched him, then her veins were a raging fire. He smacked her one more time, causing her to wriggle against him. Maybe even an inferno, because that was what he felt as he witnessed the pleasure contorting her features when he spanked her with the necklace. The reaction drove him wild with desire, so he swatted her one more time, and she cried out.

"Now, straddle me, so I can see what other tricks I can perform with these pearls."

* * *

She lowered herself across his thighs, her legs spread wide open, the skirt of her dress hiked up to her hips, her pussy exposed and aching. And he knew it. He knew she was squirming for him.

"Tricks? You're a magician now?" she said in her playfully taunting tone as she positioned herself on him.

"You tell me if it's magic when I make you come with these pearls. Close your eyes, Julia," he said, his voice deep and rumbly, sending hot shivers across her skin. The little hairs on her arms rose as the world around her disappeared. They were flying high, shooting across the country, maybe over Pennsylvania, maybe Ohio. Who knew? Who cared? They were tangoing with the sky, traveling in a silver bullet of bliss as he teased her flesh with the necklace. The sensation from the rope of pearls now gliding across her chest sent tingles over her skin. She felt his strong hands somehow wrap the pearls in a figure eight around her breasts. He tightened the strand, and she yelped in surprise, in pleasure, in the strangely thrilling sensation of having her breasts squeezed by pearls.

"Does that *ouch* mean *more please*?" he asked, low and husky in her ear.

"So. Much. More," she answered.

"Good," he said, his breath ghosting hot over her throat as he shifted the beads again, letting them fall between her breasts. He trailed them against her belly, then dropped them lower, and lower still, until the end of the loop brushed her clit with the barest whisper of a kiss. She trembled from the sweet, exquisite agony of a kiss from a pearl.

Soon she felt the pad of his finger too, pressing lightly against one of the beads, increasing the friction, rubbing up and down over her swollen clit.

She didn't know if it was the pressure from his hand, or the crazy, new sensation of the smooth object that sent a fresh rush of heat to her core. But she stopped trying to figure it out as his finger dipped down to her folds, sliding across her, and drawing out more slickness. "You're dripping on my hands. That didn't take long," he said.

"Are you disappointed with the speed of my arousal?"

"Never. It feeds me. It makes me want to see how far I can go with you, how much I can bring out in you."

"Try me then. Test me," she said, her voice as bare as her emotions for him. She was his; she belonged to him so completely. In the last two months they'd fallen deeper in love and further into pleasure, seeking out new ways to please each other. "Bring out more in me. I am yours to play with."

He bent his head to her chest, drawing a nipple into his talented mouth all while readjusting the pearls. With her eyes closed, she wasn't quite sure where he was going next. As his tongue stroked her nipple to a hard pebble, she felt strands slide lightly across her pussy, a deliciously new sensation that made her gasp.

"More," she whispered, as she held onto his strong shoulders.

"Always more," he said, gliding the pearls across her wetness. She quivered all over, her body greedy, her mind curious as to what he planned next. Where would he go with the necklace? How far would he explore her body with this smooth, sensuous piece of jewelry that was turning her inside out with pleasure under his masterful hands? Eagerly, she waited for his next move, her body hungry. Then she felt the pearls more distinctly; he'd looped them into double strands, and was sliding them across her wet, eager lips, each strand caressing her most sensitive center. A loud moan escaped her, unbidden, filling the cabin. Then another as he dragged the necklace faster through her wetness, sometimes narrowing the distance between the strands, sometimes widening them, but always making sure pearls were rubbing her where she wanted them most. All the while he continued lavishing her breasts with attention, drawing one nipple deep into his mouth, then turning to the other to lick and kiss and suck. She threw her head back as pleasure pulsed in her, like blinding bursts of white light. It was almost too much to keep up with—her breasts being fondled by his talented mouth, her hot center being stimulated with jewels.

He kept it up, rubbing the pearls between her legs, then down to the outline of her ass, touching her cheeks, then back to her desperately needy clit. She was teetering on the brink, hovering on some new precipice. But she needed more of *him* to fly over the edge.

"It feels so fucking good," she said in a breathy pant. "But I don't know if I can come without your fingers or your tongue."

"You can, Julia. I know your body. I know your arousal. I want you to come just from the pearls," he said, his voice commanding, and sending a charge through her spine. "I know you can."

"Then put them inside me," she said, the words falling out more quickly than she'd expected them to. But somehow, she knew that was what she needed to gallop over the cliff she was nearing. She wanted to launch herself over it, fling herself down the abyss of pleasure.

In a flash, she felt him pushing several beads inside her, her molten center greedily taking the friction. "Oh God," she moaned. "Yes, do that again. Please. Please, Clay. Please," she said, and soon the word had become a chant —*please*—and somehow the repetition sent her tumbling into a delirious swirl of new sensations: his finger inside her, the smoothness of the beads hitting her tight walls, then the friction, the oh-so-fucking intoxicating friction against her clit as he rubbed one bead faster and faster. Soon, her belly tightened, her sex clenched, and her sounds intensified.

She could feel the orgasm start to crest. It was almost there, nearly ready for her to bathe in its glory.

He pushed the pearls deeper inside her, and she shouted his name. Then, mere seconds later as she hovered torturously on that hazy edge, he tugged the necklace out of her quickly. The wicked feeling of the pearls leaving her body sent her soaring as she shattered with a cry that she was sure the pilot could hear. She was equally sure she didn't care about anything but the white-hot orgasm that stole her mind now as she relinquished all control, all rational thought, all of everything to her climax. This orgasm owned her body, claimed every single nerve inside her, taking her hostage in its absolute and pure bliss.

When she opened her eyes, she gripped his shoulders harder, needing to steady herself because she felt like she had no control over her body anymore. Like she'd simply sway because pleasure had consumed her, lapping her up from her head to her toes. She looked at her man, and his deep brown eyes were primal and hungry. "Get on me now, Julia. And put on your seatbelt; this is going to be a bumpy ride," he said, and she obliged instantly, sliding onto his rock-hard cock. She inhaled sharply, her breath catching as she sank down onto him, never growing tired of the way he filled her. Only this time . . . wait . . . it was different . . . there was something between them. They both looked down at the same moment, their foreheads touching.

The necklace was looped around the base of his shaft, forming a makeshift cock ring. The rest of the necklace hung below, nearly, but not quite, touching the floor. He reached down, quickly tugging up the strand of pearls the other direction, trailing it between her breasts, but leaving it on his cock, stroking in and out of her, as he held onto the necklace.

"There's a pearl necklace between us," she said, enjoying the double entendre.

"I'll gladly give you both kinds anytime," he said as he thrust into her, his strong hips and legs guiding his shaft upward, deeper, harder as she rode him.

She hitched in a breath, then her eyes widened as she watched him bring the necklace to his mouth and suck on the beads that had been inside her. Her bones turned liquid, her body became molten. He had no hang-ups, no qualms. He simply savored every single aspect of sex with her, loved every taste, every touch, every *feel*.

"You taste fucking spectacular on this necklace," he growled, his tongue lashing out across a bead to draw up her wetness. "This makes me want to bury my face between your legs, again. Julia. I can't get enough of you."

Her lips parted and she cried out as he licked the taste of her off the pearls.

So erotic, so dirty, so very, very *Clay*.

"Share with me," she said, her voice breathy as she raced to another climax. She felt it closing in on her, circling her like flames, and she wanted to ride over that edge with him this time. Jump off that cliff together and sail down on a parachute of pleasure.

Holding several pearls between his teeth, he moved his mouth to hers, claiming her lips in a fury, letting her suck on the beads with him. Their tongues lashed, their teeth banged, and together they licked off the last drops of her first orgasm as she crashed into another one. A torrent of heat, and light, and fire raced through her body, consuming her. A rush of vibrations enveloped all her cells, radiating through her blood.

The necklace fell from their mouths as he pumped deeper. His shoulders shuddered, and she could feel his climax begin. "Fuck, Julia. I fucking love coming in you. I love it. So," he said with a hard drive. "Fucking." Then another pump. "Much," he shouted, unleashing himself in her, then owning her mouth in a deep, passionate kiss, their lips united once more as their bodies connected.

As the aftershocks still chased her, she ran her fingers across his chest. "Welcome to the Mile High Club. I hope you enjoyed your flight."

He flashed a quick smile at her, then kissed her softly between her breasts, traveling up her neck, before leaving a gentle kiss on her cheek. "Makes me want to get my own jet and take you everywhere with me."

"I'll be your partner in that kind of crime."

"With you and me, it would never be a crime."

* * *

He washed off the pearls carefully, running soap and water over the necklace, then drying it off with a cotton towel. He returned to Julia who'd freshened up too, pulling on a short-sleeve blouse and a dressy pair of jeans and heels for her meeting with Farrell. She held two glasses of clear liquid, with ice cubes clinking in them. "Want to go wild and have a drink in the afternoon? Well, it's afternoon in New York at least."

He nodded. "Afternoon delight and afternoon drinks with my woman. Those are the ingredients for my perfect day."

Tucking the pearls back into the box, he glanced up at her. "I want you to wear these when we go to Brent's comedy club later tonight."

"And you'll look at me all night with lust and secrets in your eyes, knowing where they've been."

He winked. "Exactly. That's exactly what will be running through my mind every time I look at you," he said.

They settled back into their seats, Julia kicking up her shoes on the wide footrest in front of her. "Can we take this jet back to New York on Sunday night?"

"I believe that is already the plan."

"You spoil me."

"I intend to spoil you even more," he said, lacing his fingers through hers and squeezing her hand. An image flashed through his mind of how her ring finger would look with a diamond on it. Beautiful, perfect, and *his*.

"Let's watch a movie for the rest of the flight. I have *Ocean's Eleven* on my iPad."

"How fitting. Let's just hope we don't run into a ton of trouble in Vegas like they did."

"But they got away with it."

"Then if we get into trouble at a casino, I want to have the same luck on our side that they did."

Two satisfying hours later, the movie ended the way it always did—with eleven thieves walking away from the fountains at the Bellagio, one by one, having gotten away with the heist, luck on their side.

Soon the jet touched down in Vegas. Julia shook her head and smiled as she unbuckled her seatbelt. "I can't believe you're dropping me off in Vegas. On a jet. How did this become my life?"

"When you made the very wise decision to hit on me in your bar one night in San Francisco."

She laughed, the sweet sound washing over him. "Right. That's how it happened. I just jumped on you and gave you no choice."

"Or maybe I hit on you," he mused playfully, as he stood up and carried her bag to the steps of the jet. "Either way, it all worked out. I'll see you soon. Don't do anything I wouldn't do."

"That leaves things pretty much wide open."

* * *

When the Cessna landed in Los Angeles thirty minutes later, he gathered up his laptop and phone. But he couldn't find his purple tie. He searched under the seats, on the seats, even in the bathroom. It was nowhere to be found, and he texted Julia, hoping she had it.

She replied that it wasn't in her luggage or her purse, and that she was enjoying the view of the Strip from the penthouse at the Allegro.

He was glad she liked the room, but suddenly his mind stayed fixed on his damn tie. Maybe it was irrational, maybe he was superstitious, but he had the sinking feeling that his luck was running out.

CHAPTER FIVE

Friday, 1:33 p.m., Las Vegas

Julia's red-soled heels clicked against the black-and-white marbled floor of the Allegro lobby—though lobby hardly felt like the right word. The entryway was stretched out like a palace, with two giant wings that wrapped around the circular hotel creating a long, tall oval in the middle of the Strip. She'd read up on the design, and the architect had waxed eloquently about being inspired by infinity pools and wanting to create that same sort of feeling of *circularity*, he'd called it. More like trickery.

Julia suspected the design had more to do with the ease of being swallowed up in the casino, sliding quarters into slots, slapping down chips on tables, and never being able to find your way out. This hotel typified that Vegas mentality of *keep them inside*. But it did so elegantly because the walls were adorned with art, replicas of some of the very paintings inside the Allegro Gallery in the heart of this hotel that boasted authenticated works from masters like Monet, Goya and Matisse.

Gorgeous emerald-green plants and small, potted trees lined the walls too, offering an inviting feel and sending the message that this was both a welcoming and an opulent place to stay.

Lord knew their room was stunning, and seemed to go on for miles. Earlier, she'd run her hands along the royal-blue comforter and leather headboard on the king-size bed, and was then drawn to the full-length glass windows that looked over the city: all of Vegas, all of gambling, all its secrets spread out below them.

She'd sighed happily, drinking in this city. Being here was like a second chance. She and Vegas used to be bedfellows, happily in love and lust when she'd taken girls weekend trips here, playing the tables at the nearby Bellagio late into the night. But then Charlie the mobster had forced her to be his ringer and to hustle for him in rigged poker games in San Francisco to pay off her deadbeat ex-boyfriend's debt. That had sapped her love of the game just the teensiest, tiniest bit. She'd reclaim it this weekend; she'd already started taking poker back for herself, playing in New York games with Clay and Cam and a rotating cast of actors, producers, and friends. Now and then even Michelle Milo joined them. That woman had grown on her; they'd had a brief heart-to-heart when she moved to town, Julia thanking Michelle for giving Clay some of the advice he'd needed, and Michelle thanking Julia for making him—her good friend—so happy.

Here in the perfectly-modulated, precisely temperature-controlled hotel, she made her way to meet Tad Herman from Farrell Spirits at the poolside bar. The meeting wouldn't start for another twenty-five minutes, so after she passed a painting of Monet's *Japanese Bridge*, she turned into the casino in the center of the hotel, weaving her way through the tables, the flurry of quarters, nickels and dimes from the slots becoming the casino soundtrack. This sound was the music of gambling, of bets being laid, of chances being lost and won. It was the song of hope, of hands rubbed together as one-armed bandits were pulled, the players longing for the metal splash of money.

When she reached the poker tables, she scanned for one with a $25 minimum. Not too small potatoes, but nowhere near a high-roller location. She settled in with two other players, an older couple, both decked out in matching Hawaiian shirts and sipping on gigantic Pina Coladas.

Placing a $100 bill on the green felt of the table, she nodded a hello to the dealer. He was dressed in a simple yet classy black shirt with a tan vest. "Change please."

He slid four green-and-white chips to her, tucked the cash into a drawer, and began dealing.

"Welcome to our game. We're celebrating our thirtieth anniversary," the woman said in a cheery voice, flashing a bright smile at Julia.

Raising an invisible glass, Julia toasted to the couple. "To another thirty. The best is yet to come," she said.

The woman dropped her hand on top of her husband's, bumping shoulders with him and planting a kiss on his cheek. Julia smiled to herself, glad that her poker companions were a happy couple rather than a coterie of Charlie's plants, brought in to pad the game as she took down unsuspecting high-rollers. There was none of that here. She was playing without a net, playing for fun.

The way it should be.

* * *

He watched from a set of stairs by the entrance to the private club. The steps were bathed in the soft, golden glow from the bar lighting. Blending into the scenery in his Allegro-issued pit boss dress-pants and shirt, one hip rested against the brass railing on the stairs as he folded his arms over his sturdy chest.

The redhead was here.

He'd known she was coming. He'd gotten word from the front desk. She was on a list—a list that he checked regu-

larly, and had his associates monitor too. A known hustler, she was one of the most wanted in the country. Rumor was that she had some kind of magic touch. Could take down nearly anyone. She was probably a card counter, too. He'd get closer soon enough, see if he could pick up on the telltale signs from her eyes. The very best card counters were hard to pinpoint, that was the point; their leopard spots blended into a thousand other leopards, whether it was the fanny packs on their waists to appear like other tourists, or the high-class designer clothes to seem like the big spenders. But if you knew what you were looking for, if you studied those bastards closely, you could find the cheating in their eyes, and in their foreheads. The Botoxed effect, he called it, because that kind of rocket-speed counting came from intense concentration. Their eyes would be steady, and focused, their brain fixed on numbers, and the net effect of that was visible in the forehead—no furrowed brows in the best of the best. They counted without the evidence on their face, so the evidence lay in the frozen stoicism of their features.

It was all the easier to blend in when you were engaged in conversation with tablemates, and this hot piece of work had made fast friends with the silver-haired couple in their palm-treed shirts. Had she known them already? Were they her sidekicks? Plants to camouflage her hustle? He'd have to talk to the dealer later; see if he picked up on anything from her. For now, she was flashing wide smiles full of straight white teeth to the couple at her table. Then, she turned her focus back to her cards, appraising her hand, and laying down a bet.

Ten minutes later, she'd doubled her money, scooped up eight green-and-white chips, and waved goodbye to the couple. He pressed a finger against the Bluetooth device in his ear, quickly ringing up one of his colleagues.

"I need you to keep an eye on her. See where she goes."

"Yes, sir."

He hung up without another word.

Tucking the chips into a small purse, the redhead walked away from the table, her fine ass in those tight blue jeans looking quite the fodder for a shower jerk. He bet she liked it hard. He bet she liked things done to that fantastic ass. He'd love to yank down those jeans, run his hands over her smooth flesh, give her some of what he had packing. She'd probably never had it as good as what he could do.

Then he nearly smacked his wandering mind. He wasn't here for his dick. He had a job to do, and she was getting in the way of it.

CHAPTER SIX

Friday, 2:12 p.m., Las Vegas

A light breeze rippled across the cool blue waters of the pool, sleek and elegant with dark stone and classy wooden lounge chairs that surrounded it. A wrought-iron fence on one end sealed off the rooftop pool, but you could peer over it six stories below and watch the crowds roll by along the Strip, packs of sightseers and throngs of conventioneers jamming down the sidewalks of the city, popping in and out of the hotels and shopping malls that beckoned to them.

The warm air rustled her hair, blowing a few strands across her cheek. She pushed back, then took a drink of her iced tea. Tad had an iced water. She wasn't surprised that he wasn't drinking. It was a business meeting, after all. What surprised her was his teetotaling attitude. When the waitress had stopped by the high table where they perched on cushions on bamboo stools, he'd held up his hands and waved off the idea of liquor like it was a virus.

"Oh no, I never drink," he'd said.

Julia had wanted to make a joke about his age, but she'd bit her tongue. He did look like his mom drove him to the meeting—he had a tiny nose, the smooth, baby-face of a pre-teen and the skinny body of a boy barely in puberty. Add in the towhead blond hair, and she'd have carded him in a heartbeat at Speakeasy. But she knew from researching him in advance that he was twenty-nine, and the son of the company's chief marketing officer.

She'd gleaned too, from spending a few minutes with him that he was serious. *Intensely* serious. He placed his hands together, and she did the same. Tad's all-business persona made her mirror him: serious, straightforward, and focused.

"As you know, Ms. Bell," he began, and Julia stifled a small laugh, because no one ever called her *Ms. Bell*. "We want to expand your role at Farrell Spirits. The Purple Snow Globe has been a big hit." He proceeded to rattle off numbers and percentages that thrilled her. She was proud of her drink-baby; consumers loved it, and stores had picked it up and stocked it, then sold out of it.

"I am delighted that it's been doing right by you, and I so appreciate you taking a chance on my drink."

He held up his hands in deference. "No chance taken there. You deserve all the credit for creating it. In fact, our market research tells us that consumers both love the drink, and you. They want to know more about you."

She raised an eyebrow. "Market research about me?"

"Not exactly about you. But the beverage, and what they like. Of course, they love the taste, but they also like you—the article Glen Mills ran about discovering your drink was one of the most popular in his magazine and drove hundreds of thousands of views online. We've been tracking the reviews and write-ups in blogs and across cocktail sites for those who try the drink in person at Speakeasy in New York. The bottom line is—they want more of you."

"Why on earth would someone want more of me?"

He furrowed his brow at her as if her question didn't compute. He reached inside his briefcase, took out a stack of papers, and stabbed his finger at it. "Because they call you *the beautiful bartender.* Because they like your . . ." He paused to read the notes again. ". . . charm. Your confidence. Your conversations."

He looked up as an extremely tall man in a black suit passed behind the table, sunglasses shielding his eyes. "After crunching the numbers and running a P&L, we've concluded that we can grow the Purple Snow Globe business significantly if the drink and you become synonymous," he said linking his fingers together as if to demonstrate.

She couldn't resist. She simply couldn't not touch that. "So they want to drink me?" she asked in a sexy purr.

A blush crossed over his baby cheeks. "I'm sorry. I didn't mean it like that."

Poor guy. She'd been too bawdy when this young man clearly needed the safe-for-work Julia. "No, it's okay. My apologies."

He took a deep breath, perhaps recalibrating. "So, we'd like you to appear in some ads, in the marketing materials, maybe even a TV spot, and on the packaging. We think it can help skyrocket the product even further, and we're prepared to pay handsomely for the additional role we'd be asking you to take on," he said, then shared a number that nearly made her jaw drop. But she'd mastered the poker face long ago, and it came in handy here as she gave a curt nod and let him continue. "There's only one stipulation," he said, then cleared his throat.

Ah, the fine print. There was always a hoop to jump through. "And that stipulation is?"

"It's a morals clause," he said, in a firm tone.

"Morals? I'm a good girl," she said, reverting back to jokes. But inside, she started spinning. Why on earth would he be concerned about her morals?

"I'm sure you're pristine, but the reason I bring this up is we are a spirits company, and while that may seem on the surface that we're loose and fast, we actually have to be quite buttoned-up about the law, and the rules."

"I assure you, Tad. I am over twenty-one," she said, flashing him a playful smile, because what the hell was he hinting at?

He returned her smile, not showing any teeth. "I am referring to who you associate with. The people you consort with. As I understand, you were involved with Dillon Whittaker, and he is now in prison for tax evasion," he said. Her shoulders tightened and she gritted her teeth just from hearing the name of her ex. The fucker was finally behind bars where he belonged and she so did not need him messing with her future.

"Dillon is not a part of my life at all," she said crisply.

Tad nodded. "That is good to hear. Our spokespeople need to be above reproach. We would still like you to sign this morals clause to ensure that you uphold a proper reputation, including but not limited to no public intoxication, and no involvement with any sort of criminal element."

She held her breath, waiting for him to breathe Charlie's name, the mobster she'd previously owed money to. But perhaps only the Dillon connection had been flagged? Would Farrell have any way of knowing that she'd pretty much been in the mob's back pocket when she lived in San Francisco? She'd had no choice, of course. She wasn't a mob wife—she was a woman who'd been screwed over by an ex and had clawed her way out of that trouble. She resented the implication that she was a cause for concern for Farrell, so she strapped on her best tough-chick smile, and said, "I am squeaky clean, Mr. Herman. You don't have to worry about me."

She took the papers and said farewell to him as he gathered his bag and phone. As soon as he was out of sight, she ordered a big, fat drink. She crossed her arms over her chest, still huffing at Tad's not-so-subtle finger-jabbing.

She stared at the water, trying to let it calm her, and the cool sheet of blue soon became a balm to her frustrations. The sun beat down overhead, warming her skin, and reminding her to let it go. Tad's attitude wasn't what mattered here. She had a golden chance to expand her role as a business partner with Farrell and she'd be downright exemplary. She wasn't a criminal, she didn't have a record, and she played by the rules.

She uncrossed her arms and breathed out, imagining her frustrations blowing away in the breeze.

She surveyed the other pool-goers, mostly packs of single women in barely-there bikinis and groups of bachelor-party-esque men moving in to hit on them. Off in the distance she noticed someone who didn't fit either bill—the tall man in the suit who'd walked past her table earlier. He was parked on the other side of the pool, alone: no iPad in front of him, no phone in his hands, and dressed for the shade rather than the sun. She couldn't tell where he was looking, but when her spine tingled like a warning, she had the distinct feeling that he was watching her. His attire reminded her of Charlie, who'd dressed in black suits. Was he part of Charlie's crew? Maybe the Vegas arm of his operations?

Oh shit.

Her mind went racing at sixty miles per hour. Charlie had to have sent someone to check up on her. In a flash, she rose from the stool, and made her way out of the pool area, and into an indoor hall, forgetting about the waiter bringing her the drink. As nerves prickled over her skin, she picked up the pace, making a beeline for the elevators. Glancing behind her once, her eyes latched onto a flash of black fabric, then it was gone. She spun around, hunting for the man in the suit who'd been watching her. Where was he? She didn't see him anywhere.

Maybe he'd darted down a dark hallway out of sight. Perhaps, he was lying in wait for her. Ready to pounce.

She picked up the pace.

Maybe she was overreacting. Maybe she was imagining things, but heart was beating a frantic rhythm. As soon as she reached the room, she called Clay, locking the door, and bolting it shut as his number rang.

CHAPTER SEVEN

Friday, 2:36 p.m., Los Angeles

He hated ignoring Julia, but his client was in tears.

Tears of happiness, but still. He didn't want to be a dick, and cut Grant off while the man was having his moment. Besides, Julia was probably calling to share good news about her Farrell meeting, and good news could keep for five more minutes.

"Grant, I couldn't be happier for you. This is what we wanted—to get you back in the saddle," Clay said as the cab driver dodged and darted L.A. traffic.

"My wife is crying too. She's so damn happy," Grant said in a blubbery voice that pulled even harder at Clay's heartstrings.

"I'm just sorry we couldn't get Comedy Nation to go up. Had to take a bit of a hit on some points, but Gino's a tough one," Clay said, deliberately softening his report on the negotiations. Gino wasn't merely a tough one— that was a euphemism. Gino was an asshole. A grade-A, top-choice, piece of fucking work that reminded him of an angry gorilla in a suit. Come to think of it, Gino looked a bit like a gorilla too with hair everywhere. Clay chuckled to himself at that picture, and it did wonders to tamp down his anger over being shoved into a corner during that deal.

"Don't apologize," Grant said. "I wanted this deal no matter what, and you got it for me. That's what matters. I would have taken half the money and still happily signed, so there. You should feel like you doubled my money."

Clay smiled, and already Gino's jackass ways were fading into the rearview mirror. "All right. He's sending me the contract, and I'll take a final look Monday morning and then send you a digital copy to sign. You go out and celebrate with your wife. Give her my best."

"I will. And if there's ever anything I can do for you, let me know. I owe you big time," Grant said. "Now aren't you supposed to be in Vegas this weekend?"

"I am. And I should be there in about an hour. Talk to you soon," he said, hanging up just as an email landed in his inbox from Etsy. The screen flashed the message— *Package en route to Allegro Hotel. Will bring to room by seven p.m.*

Damn.

That wouldn't do. He'd have to get back in touch with the buyer and have the box left at the front desk, as he'd specified when he placed the same-day delivery order. But first things first. He wanted to talk to Julia, so he clicked on her number.

When she answered, her voice sounded strained.

"Hey. What's wrong?"

"I honestly don't know," she said.

"Wait. Something *is* wrong?"

"No. Yes. I don't know," she said, a worried sigh following her. "I'm probably overreacting or freaking out, and you're going to laugh at me, but I promised you I'd be honest with you and not hide things," she started, and he was both thrilled that she continued to lay her heart on the line every day, but also nervous about where she was going. Words like *freaking out* and *hide things* weren't his favorites. Call him crazy, but they didn't usually signal the good stuff in life. But still, given the troubles they'd had in the past over truths and lies, he needed to be supportive.

"What is it Julia? I'm not going to laugh," he said gently, as the cab hopped over a lane, then sped down the exit ramp leading to the Van Nuys airport where the jet was waiting for him.

"Okay, so I was just with Tad from Farrell at the pool-side bar, and when the meeting ended I had the weirdest sensation that there was a guy watching me."

"I take it you mean more than checking you out because you're the most beautiful woman in the entire city of sin?"

She didn't even laugh at his compliment, or sass him back. "No. I felt his eyes on me. Like the guy was watching me and following me, Clay. When I left and walked down the hallway to the elevators, I swore he was behind me. I turned around, but he must have moved so quickly because then he was gone."

"Well that's good that he was gone," Clay said as they passed a sign for the airport.

"But do you think . . ." she said, letting her voice trail off and he knew what she meant.

"That it was one of Charlie's men?" he supplied.

"Maybe?" she offered up, uncertain, unsure.

"I doubt it, Julia. Charlie, strangely enough, is a man of his word. He said he'd leave you alone. Was it just hotel security, maybe?"

"Maybe," she said but didn't sound convinced. "I did sit down at one of the poker tables before the meeting. Met a sweet couple from Florida celebrating their anniversary. I played a few hands and won all of them, and they didn't even blanch when I took their money. Even asked me to teach them how to play better."

He laughed. "Of course you won. And now the Allegro is probably watching out for the newest poker shark in town, so the casino will have eyes on you."

"I suppose it was nothing then," she said, and she seemed to believe it this time.

"It has to be nothing. There's no reason for anyone to follow you. Besides, Charlie's been expanding into New York, and we've never had any trouble there. I don't want you to worry, and I would never say you're worrying for nothing, but I think it's just that this hotel is teeming with security. Brent even told me so. New hotel, high-end, lots of money coming through. He has some friends that run security firms in Vegas and they were practically tripping over themselves to get the contract. His buddy won the contract though, so let me call Brent, and I'm sure he'll say the same. That it's nothing but the hotel having extra precautions with all the attention it's getting," he said, swaying to the right as the driver took a sharp turn on the road to the airport.

"Okay. I'm sure that's it. I'm not going to worry about it."

"Good. Now tell me about Farrell," he said, and she gave him a brief update about meeting Tad Herman, mentioning that the guy was super concerned about making sure she was "above reproach."

"He actually used those words. *Above reproach*. And he wants me to sign a morals clause. Do you think they know about the way I used to spend my Tuesday nights?"

"You didn't sign it, did you?"

"Of course not. I do have a lawyer, you know."

"Good. And to answer your question, no. I seriously doubt they know about the rigged games. I would just assume they are trying to cover their own asses. They've probably gotten burned in the past."

"That makes sense. I just really want this. It's a great chance for me to grow my career. Capitalize on what I've built already."

"I guess we should make sure you don't land yourself in jail then," he teased.

"Would you break me out from behind bars if I did?"

"I would break you out, but only after I'd had my way with you through the bars," he said.

She drew a sharp breath. "*Clay.*"

Her quick arousal fueled him as it always did. "I'd find you in your solitary cell, looking all forlorn and wanting to get out, and I'd promise to pay your bail on one condition."

"And what would that condition be?" she asked, her voice quickly turning breathy.

"That you let me touch you through the bars."

"I would agree to that. I would definitely let you do that."

"Yeah? You'd hike up your skirt for me in jail, Julia?"

"Yes, and I'd make it worth your while. You'd have your hands on the bars, watching me, and I'd drive you wild, giving you a little peek of my ass, then turning back around and lifting my skirt just a little bit."

A hot wave of desire rumbled through him as he pictured the scene. "Come closer to the bars, let me touch that sweet little body of yours when you're all locked up."

"And you're the key to get me out and get me off," she purred.

"You better have your hand in your panties right now, Julia," he growled, not caring if the cab driver was listening, not giving a shit at all because his woman was turned on. Far be it from him to leave her unsatisfied whether he was there to service her or not.

"I'm ahead of you, Mister. I stripped off my jeans when you said *have your way with me*. I'm lying on the hotel bed, with my legs wide open and my fingers slip sliding away," she said, and he closed his eyes as if the image was almost too much to take.

"I hate the thought of your beautiful naked body ready to be fucked, and that I'm not there to do it. So I need you to lift up that skirt to your hips and bring your sweet pussy closer to me. Let me finger you behind bars."

She moaned loudly, the sound of her desire washing over him. "I'm taking off my panties, handing them to you through the bars. You're sniffing them, like you like to do."

"Like I *love* to do," he corrected, and he was tempted, so tempted to stroke his raging hard-on. He resisted, focusing instead on pleasing her three hundred miles away. "And then I'd slide my fingers up your legs, rub them across your wet pussy and make you rock into my hand."

"Yes," she cried out. "I want to fuck your hand through the bars."

"I'll be holding onto one of the bars, and the other will be up your skirt. I'd rub your sweet clit with my thumb and then fuck you with my fingers, filling you that way," he said, picturing her riding his hand shamelessly. "Rock into my hand, ride it, straddle it. Come all over my hand, Julia."

"Oh God," she said, her voice hitting that perfect pitch that signaled her orgasm. "Oh God, Clay. I'm coming in your hand right now. All fucking over you."

"That's right. Because that's your bail, and that's the only way I'm letting you out of your cell; when you give me your orgasm," he said, in a low and dirty voice, as her moans filled his ears, the most beautiful music there ever was.

"I'm giving it to you," she panted, and then moaned happily. "Over and over, and many, many times," she said, and he could hear the purr in her voice, and he imagined her stretching out sexily on the bed, all glowing and sated.

He wished he could say the same for himself. What he wouldn't give to bury his cock in her right now and fuck her relentlessly. "When I get back to the hotel in an hour and a half, I'm going to need you on your hands and knees, Julia. So consider this your warning," he said, as the cab slowed to a stop.

"That'll be twenty-eight dollars," the driver said with a completely straight face. Clay caught his reflection in the rearview mirror. Good man. He hadn't been bothered by the dirty talk. Handing him a fifty, he said, "Keep the change."

When the cab pulled away, he returned his focus to Julia. "I'm at the airport now. I'll see you soon. Expect to get fucked good."

"Nothing less, Clay. Nothing less."

* * *

The purposeful stride across the small terminal, the serious look on Greg Barton's face, and the eyes that spelled bad news told him everything he needed to know before the man opened his mouth.

Well, maybe not *everything*. Not the specifics. But as soon as the pilot started speaking, Clay already knew the flight wasn't taking off on time.

"There's a problem with the landing gear. It looked like we were all set to go, but maintenance did a final check and found some trouble. The part should be here in about an hour and a half, then we'll need a bit of time to fix it."

His jaw clenched, reflexively. He was tired of bad news. But he wasn't going to dwell on it. He stroked his chin, contemplating options. "What are the chances of arranging for another jet? Is that a possibility?"

Greg shook his head, and sighed heavily. "I already checked into that. I called Frederick Pinkerton's assistant, and she said she could arrange for a charter on another jet but that would likely take the same amount of time."

"Commercial then?"

The pilot shrugged, frowning. "Burbank's the closest airport. But at this time of day," he said, holding his hands out wide as if to say *no go*, "you're looking at bumper-to-bumper just getting there."

Clay muttered a curse under his breath. "So that leaves me stuck here for a couple hours?"

"'Fraid so. If you want to kick back in the executive lounge, make some calls, even have a meal or a drink, you've got some time."

"Thanks," he said, clenching his fists because that wasn't what he wanted to do whatsoever. First, he wanted to see his woman, he wanted to touch his woman, and he wanted to fuck his woman. Then he wanted to take her to see his brother's show, go to a club, dance with her in a dark corner, and do all those first things a second time. Then a third time.

This weekend was not going as he'd planned. That pissed him off, and though he was all about being flexible and rolling with the punches, he'd already been served up the big fat curveball in the form of Gino. Another one was not cool. Reflexively, he reached for his tie to adjust it out of habit, but his hand found buttons instead.

Right. His lucky tie was missing.

"Hey Greg," he called out. "Did you happen to find a purple tie on the plane?"

"I didn't notice one, but let me go take a look now."

Greg returned to the tarmac while Clay spun around, assessing the surroundings at the Van Nuys airport. A small coffee bar, boasting fresh-roasted Four Barrel Coffee, a plush seating area with leather chairs and glossy magazines with golf courses and yachts on the covers, a rental car counter, and an information desk. He pulled out his phone and did a quick search for commercial flights, but the next one out of Burbank didn't leave until six. Even then it wasn't direct. If he caught the seven p.m. flight, he'd land in Vegas by eight. He looked up, thinking, running through his options. His eyes returned to the rental car counter, and he shrugged to himself. Why not? At this rate, a car might be faster. Van Nuys wasn't far from the 15, and that should be a straight shot in a little more than four hours. He'd likely arrive sooner.

He headed over to the Hertz sign, and inquired about rentals and the best route to Vegas. The woman behind the counter gave him the necessary details.

"Give me one minute," he said to her and headed for the doors leading to the tarmac. He spotted Greg outside the Cessna, chatting with a mechanic. When they were done, he waved the pilot over.

Clay clapped him on the upper arm and lowered his voice. He didn't want the whole world to know he was superstitious. If the tie had been located, he'd wait here. If it was still AWOL then it was time to cut bait from the cursed plane. "Did you find that tie?"

Greg shook his head ruefully. "Sorry. Scoured the whole cabin."

"All right. Decision's made then. I'll be driving to Vegas. Thank you very much for getting me to Los Angeles safely."

Greg saluted him, and Clay was glad the man didn't quibble, didn't try to insist. An air force pilot, he surely understood the need to make quick decisions and stand by them. "Have a safe drive, sir. I'll have the plane back in Vegas tonight for your return to New York on Sunday night."

"Thank you," he said, then rented a car. As he signed the necessary documents, a strange thought flashed through his brain. Had Greg delayed the flight on purpose? With lightning speed, the pilot had knocked down all the alternatives Clay had suggested. As if he were trying to keep him from Julia.

His blood slowed and his mind whirred as he considered the possibilities. Could Greg be working for Charlie? Nah. No way that could be the case. Because if he worked for Charlie, how would he just happen to be flying the Pinkertons' plane? That'd be too much of a coincidence. But then, Charlie had contacts everywhere, and inside men all over the country. Charlie ran the underworld of San Francisco. He knew how to get things done, down to infiltrating Clay's life with a pilot. Was Charlie making a move on Julia in Vegas? Keeping him away from her by any means possible so he could go after her in his absence? Was the man in the hotel somehow connected to Greg? To Charlie?

The thought of her three hundred miles away from him made his stomach churn.

No. He slammed on the mental brakes. He had to stop this train of thought. He was getting worked up over nothing. Greg Barton was a military man, not a mob insider. Greg had no vendetta against him, he reminded himself, as he walked to the parking lot and found his car. But as he turned the key in the ignition and backed up, Clay was adding up clues that maybe should or maybe shouldn't be added. The dark suit Greg wore. The black suit Charlie wore. The black suit the tall man in the hotel was sporting, Julia had said.

Sometimes a suit is just a suit. But sometimes it's more.

As he pulled out of the parking lot, turning on the GPS, conspiracy theories were playing havoc with his head, and he knew he needed to get to Vegas as quickly as he possibly could.

He gunned the gas and sped away.

CHAPTER EIGHT

Friday, 3:01 p.m., Las Vegas

"Did you get a name yet?" he asked as he made his rounds, strolling casually—or so it appeared—past the roulette tables. The crowds were building as more gamblers packed themselves like sardines at the games.

"Yeah. He's Tad Herman. He's a marketing executive at Farrell Spirits. Did a quick search on him. Lives in Vegas. Has for ten years. Looks like he was in some kind of trouble once, but it was several years ago back in Florida."

He scoffed as he ran a hand through his dark, gelled hair. "Florida. That place is a hotbed for crime."

His associate laughed. "Damn right it is."

"What kind of trouble?"

"Not sure. I need to do more digging."

"Well, what are you waiting for?" he said gruffly as he continued his rounds. "Get out your shovel and dig that shit up." He stabbed the end call button on his Bluetooth device as he meandered past the blackjack tables. A few feet away,

he spotted a young man in a hoodie. He slowed his pace to watch the hipster. He looked just like those MIT fuckers who bilked millions from Vegas' casino kings. Profiling, that's what he was doing, and he knew it. But profiling worked, so he kept his focus on the hoodie who might very well be on the list of known card counters. Casually reaching for his phone, he swiped his thumb across the screen and snapped a shot. He'd send it on later to his contacts, and see if he was right. He was rarely wrong. He knew gamblers, and the professional ones could never stay away from the action for long.

Like that redhead. He'd like to get another look at her, at those ripe tits that would fit so nicely in his palms. Hot as fuck and a penchant for gambling—that woman must be all kinds of fire in the sack. If she came back down to the tables, he'd be ready for her. Oh, hell, he'd be ready for her.

He licked his lips, his tongue sliding over the bottom one.

* * *

Friday, 4:07 p.m., Highway 15 en route from Los Angeles to Las Vegas

As soon as he hit the highway, the sun was blaring high in the sky, like a goddamn alien beam of light from a spaceship, designed to blind him. He dropped his shades over his eyes, shielding them from the glare through the windshield. He slid his phone into the holder on the dashboard and turned on the speaker.

First, Charlie.

He hit the call button, and the man who used to have Julia under his thumb answered on the third ring.

"Well, well, well. If it isn't the man with steel balls."

Clay did his best to force out a laugh. "Iron, actually. I had a metal transplant last month."

"Excellent news. I hope the surgeon stitched you up well," he said in his lightly accented voice. Clay heard the sounds of dishes being stacked and assumed Charlie was at his favorite place in the world—his restaurant, Mr. Pong's. "I hope you've finally come to your senses and plan to take me up on my offer of employment."

"Afraid not. The actors and producers of the world are keeping me pretty busy."

Charlie cleared his throat, stripped the casual tone from it. "So what do you want then? Or rather, what do you need? I'm watching the Giants game right now, and Buster Posey is on deck. I never miss Buster Posey at bat."

"He's your favorite player ever," Clay said, remembering the conversation they'd had about sports the one time they'd had lunch at Charlie's eatery when Clay had secured the terms for Julia's freedom. "And he's having a great season. On track for MVP."

"He is. I've got my bets down already."

"Of course you do," Clay said.

"So why are you calling?"

He'd been weighing just the right words, but wasn't even sure if the right ones existed for his question. "I don't suppose you've taken up a new interest in Julia, have you?"

Silence. He was met with stark silence, and it felt lethal. Like he'd crossed a line. Seconds later, Charlie spoke. "Why would you think I have an interest in Red?"

"Because she thought there were some people following her in Vegas," he said, figuring honesty was the best policy at this point.

"What a shame for her," Charlie said in a dry voice. Clearly, he didn't think it was a shame at all. "I hope it's not bringing her trouble but—and correct me if I'm wrong, though I'm sure I'm not—we did have a deal, right?"

Clay's chest tightened and he gripped the wheel harder, trying to keep his eyes on the road while also focusing on the conversation that was quickly going south. "Yes. We had a deal," he said.

"And I believe," Charlie began, stopping to take another harrowing pause that sent Clay's pulse racing, "that the deal was I would leave her alone if the money was paid. The money was paid, the debt was clear, and we shook hands like men. So why would you call me and ask such a question?"

Shit. His luck wasn't just gone. It was fucking being filleted, fried and served back to him on a platter.

"Hey, nothing to it. Just looking out for my woman."

"As a man should. But it saddens me that you would misconstrue the terms of our deal. I said I would leave her alone, and I have left her alone. In fact, I haven't even thought once about her. I have new ringers, all over the country, and I don't need a thing from her."

He gulped. "The country?"

"I do not want to have this conversation now, or anytime, frankly. You knew I was expanding and moving games to new cities. I have new ringers, and they are taking care of business. But you are not. You are violating business ethics. I do not like the insinuation that I would disrespect our deal. You are pissing me off."

He heaved a sigh, and prepared to eat crow for the second time that day. Grovel if he had to. But the line had gone dead. Charlie had hung up on him. His stomach dropped.

He banged his fist on the steering wheel. Great, just great. He'd made a mobster mad. He might as well have waved a flag in front of a bull.

He was about to call him back when an email flashed on his screen, again from the delivery company. Trying to keep his eyes on the road, he managed a quick glance. *En*

route for an early delivery. We expect the package to arrive at
the Allegro by five.

Fucking A.

Could anything more go awry today? First the seller was molasses slow. Now, the delivery company was far too fast.

He'd have to deal with the problems one by one. He called the delivery company, but was met with a voicemail. So not what he needed.

But then he realized he didn't need to reach them. He simply needed to reach someone who'd intercept the package. He sure as hell didn't want Julia's paws on the special gift he'd tracked down. She'd figure out somehow that it was part of a bigger gift. It was designed to be a part of the whole damn proposal, and with everything that had already been screwed sideways today, he needed the proposal to go smoothly. He wanted her to be surprised and he was using this gift to throw her off the scent. Then bam, he'd slide into home.

He dialed his little brother's number.

"Where the fuck are you? I've been dying for you to hear my new routine. It might even make *you* blush," Brent said, launching right into things, not even bothering with a hello.

"I'd expect nothing less from your filthy mouth."

"Gotta play the part, tats and bike and all."

"What would you say to getting on that bike, riding it over to the Allegro, and heading off a package coming from this delivery service before my soon-to-be fiancée gets her hands on it?"

"Aww. That's sweet that you need me to be your gopher bitch," he teased. "What's it worth to you?"

"It's worth me not smacking you upside the head when I see you tonight. How about that?"

"You always strike a fair bargain. Consider it done."

Clay cleared his throat. "And Brent, can you do me a favor? After you get the package, can you check on Julia? Maybe play a few rounds with her, buy her a drink? I won't be there for another few hours, and I don't want her to be alone," he said, laying bare his concerns.

Brent stripped the joking from his voice, clearly sensing that something was amiss. "Everything okay?"

"Yeah. I think so. But you can never be too safe right? Sometimes you get a notion that prying eyes are on your woman, and you can't shake it."

"Say no more. I'm there. I'm on my way right now," he said, and Clay could hear the clinking of keys and the shutting of the door. "Hey, how big is this package?"

"It should be in a small box, I'm guessing. It's a necklace, but I didn't want Julia to see it and think it was the ring because of the size of the box."

"All right, man. I'll drop it at the club. It's right next door to the Allegro, though next door is a nebulous term in Vegas. Then I'll go entertain your lady."

"If I didn't trust you with my life, I'd warn you not to try anything funny, but *A*, I trust you with my life and *B*, I'd beat you up, just like I did when we were kids."

"Hey! You never beat me up. I always beat you."

Clay laughed deeply. "That, my friend, is revisionist history right there."

"You remember it your way. I remember it my way. I'm going to hit the road. I'll text you when I'm there in about twenty minutes. The valets know me so parking is easy."

Know me. Clay latched onto those words. "You know the firm that runs security for the hotel?"

"That I do. My friend Mindy runs it."

"A woman?"

"You think a woman can't handle security? She's former Special Forces. She'd badass."

"I haven't got a single sexist bone in my body. I was just surprised."

"Anyway, you need me to check on something?"

"Yeah. Make sure Julia's not being followed."

"Ten-four."

Then he called Julia, letting her know he was driving instead of flying.

"Well, that sucks, because I miss you something fiercc."

"I miss you too. But I'll be there soon. And listen, Brent's coming by. Go play some poker with him, okay? I called him to have him look out for you. And before you go all stubborn and independent on me, I did it because you were worried, and when you're worried I'm worried, and even though I'm sure nothing is amiss I'm not taking any chances. Brent will make sure you feel safe."

He tensed, waiting for her to reprimand him. Instead, she made the sweetest sound. "Awww. That is so adorable. And I will happily let your brother be my security detail."

"It is? Adorable?"

"It is. And it makes me think about how far we've come. It makes me think about what almost split us up, and now here you are, laying it all out for me and telling me upfront."

His heart beat faster and he couldn't contain the smile. He dropped his foot harder on the gas, needing desperately to see his gorgeous Julia and wrap her in his arms. "And look at you. Taking my help so easily too. So different than before when you were kicking and screaming."

"We're a good team."

"Always, gorgeous. Always," he said, and he was proud of them, of how far they'd come, and how much they'd learned to trust each other. He truly felt the two of them could conquer the world.

Now, if only he could get to Vegas. He ended the call and punched a few buttons to install an app that gave alerts as to cops and speeding traps. There were none showing, so he let the speedometer crank higher, putting more distance between himself and Los Angeles.

A second later, an incoming text message from Julia flashed across his screen. A multimedia file. Oh fuck. His dick twitched just imagining what she'd sent. He glanced in the rearview mirror, then the side mirror, then made sure all was clear on the stretch of highway ahead of him. He steeled himself as he swiped his finger across the screen and nearly swerved off the side of the road when a picture of her breasts greeted him. So lush, so round, so designed for him to bite down and suck.

What do you want to do with these tonight?

He took a deep fueling breath, then spoke into the voice-recognition software, the phone transcribing his reply. "Slide my rock-hard cock between them and watch you suck the head of my dick as I fuck your breasts. That's what I want to do with them tonight. This is your fair warning."

CHAPTER NINE

Friday, 5:58 p.m., Las Vegas

He wasn't quite the spitting image of his brother, but he was damn close. Waiting by the replica of Monet's *Japanese Bridge*, she picked Brent out of the sea of people in the lobby immediately. He was tall like Clay, and stood head and shoulders above most. With thick, dark hair, piercing brown eyes, and a strong, square jawline, he'd been blessed with the same beauty stick that had tapped his brother. They must have been lady-killers in high school. She was even more eager now to meet Clay's parents in the flesh, and say hello to the two people who had created such a set of fine male specimens.

There were plenty of differences though. Brent was scruffier, edgier, and not the least bit the suit. With well-worn jeans, motorcycle boots, and a faded navy T-shirt, he and Clay would never raid each other's closets. Brent had a whole mess of stubble, and was rocking the I-don't-need-to-shave look.

"You must be the bad boy of comedy," Julia said, extending a hand when he reached her.

He shrugged playfully, his lips quirking up. "So bad he should be banned," Brent said, clasping her hand in his. "That's the slogan at my club. Now, c'mon. Give me a hug. You're my brother's woman. We're beyond handshakes even if we just met."

She smiled broadly, liking him immediately. He pulled her in close enough for her to notice his woodsy scent; maybe it was cologne, maybe it was soap. An appealing scent that was sure to send some woman to her knees. As for this woman, she only got on her knees for one man, and she was hoping that was where she'd be soon when Clay arrived. Until then, she'd happily take the company of the younger brother.

When they pulled apart, Brent tipped his forehead to the casino. "What's your poison? Craps? Roulette? Blackjack? Or you want to play the one-armed bandits? This hotel has all the new ones, so you've got options," Brent said, and began counting off on his fingers. "We've got a *Sex and the City* machine, and you need to line up three cosmos to win, or else a trio of Samantha's massagers will do. Or you can go for *Aladdin's Quest* and maybe you'll get to rub that magic lamp and watch the coins pour out. You could also sidle up to the most mind-boggling one of all—the Dolly Parton slot machine."

Julia arched an eyebrow. "Should I even ask what you need to line up to win?"

Brent held both his hands in front of his chest. "Melons," he said, punctuating the word crisply.

"Somehow, I think you might be full of it."

"Ah, see, I like you already, Julia," Brent said, draping an arm over her shoulder and guiding her through the echoing marble-floored lobby, and into the *cha-ching-clang*ing casino. Coins rained down for a lucky patron nearby and "9 to 5" began playing loudly. Julia laughed, pointing to the Dolly Parton machine at the end of the aisle, lit up with a trio of photos of the country music legend. "No melons," she said. "And by the way, I'll take blackjack for 500, Alex."

"Blackjack it is, though Clay said you were a poker fan."

"I am, but I played earlier and I am ready to mix it up and try my luck at twenty-one."

"Then off to the tables we go," he said, holding out his right arm grandly as they weaved through the evening crowds, passing a woman decked out in a little black dress, a man in a sharp suit and blue shirt, and a woman wearing flats, gray, pressed pants, and a short-sleeve white blouse, looking like a perfectly adorable second-grade teacher. The woman smiled brightly at Brent, waved at him like she hadn't seen him in years, then threw her arms around him when she reached them.

"Hey Miss Mindy, how are you?"

"Fabulous," she said in a high-pitched squeak. "And I got your text message earlier, and all is well."

"Excellent. I'll call you later for more details," he said and she nodded a yes, then he gestured to Julia. "Mindy, this is Julia Bell. She's practically part of the family. She's with Clay."

Mindy extended a hand to shake, and holy fucking smokes, she had one of the strongest grips Julia had ever felt. Brent continued the intros. "Julia, this is Mindy. She runs security here for the Allegro. I helped her get the gig."

Mindy rolled her pretty blue eyes. "Oh, you wish. You are so full of shit, Brent Nichols. I am not going to let you win at arm wrestling the next time."

Then she turned to Julia, who was watching the buddy-buddy rapport between the two of them and trying to get a read on it. "It's a pleasure to meet you," Mindy said, then wagged a finger at Julia and spoke in a faux-authoritative voice. "And don't snap any cell-phone pictures of the slot machines or I'll have to kick you out."

"And she kicks like a motherfucker. She spent ten years with Special Forces before starting her own security firm."

She waved a hand dismissively as if her reputation were no big deal, and Julia found the oxymoronic nature of this woman adorable—she was tiny and gleeful, but she sure as hell packed a punch, and now Julia knew why. A sparkle from around her neck caught Julia's attention—a brushed silver chain with a miniature antique-styled teacup hanging on it.

Like a squirrel drawn to a shiny object, Julia reached for it without thinking. "Oh my, this is so damn cute," she said, admiring the tiny charm.

"Thank you so much," Mindy said, then lowered her voice to a whisper, gesturing to her white and gray attire. "I have to dress simply and blend in, but I do like to add a little accent for fun."

"It reminds me of something I saw on my sister's show," Julia said, then quickly explained. "She's a fashion blogger, and she loves vintage and retro clothes and jewelry."

"Show?" Mindy's voice rose with the sound of hope.

"She has a video show called *The Fashion Hound*."

Mindy's blue eyes turned into those of a cartoon character, nearly popping out of her head, boinging and bouncing on coiled springs of disbelief. "I. Love. That. Show. I follow it like it's a religion. She's my guilty pleasure. She did an episode recently on vintage jewelry and talked about these necklaces."

"That is so cool," Julia said. "I can't wait to tell her I ran into a fan of hers."

"Please tell her my dream is for her to be my fashion consultant for pretty little accessories."

"She will be delighted to hear that."

Then Mindy's face turned serious, and she seemed to be focusing on something. She raised her hand to her right ear, pressing on a Bluetooth piece, then spoke in a low voice. "Be right there."

Pointing vaguely in the opposite direction, she said, "I need to go take care of something, but it was so great meeting you, Julia. And Brent, I will kick your ass the next time I see you and that's a promise."

She saluted Brent and picked up the pace as she walked away.

"She's sweet," Julia remarked.

"Yeah, she's the best. Just don't cross her," Brent said playfully, but also in an admiring tone that made her realize he was being truthful. Julia made a mental note—don't mess with Mindy.

* * *

What the hell?

Now she was using the brother connection as a cover-up for her hustling? Wearing a tight little skirt, a strappy tank, and a long string of pearls, she sashayed up to a blackjack dealer, cashed in for chips, and then commanded the whole damn table. She brought along that wise-ass comedian. Stupid joker acted like he was Vegas royalty, strutting around like a big man on campus.

He knew all about Julia, knew every last detail, down to who she lived with, and she was fucking this smart aleck's brother. Now, he was seeing how she operated, bringing in locals to make herself seem clean.

No wonder she was at the top of the list.

He brought a glass of water to his lips, and downed it one thirsty gulp. Fucking desert. This place was so goddamn dry, and he was always parched. Plunking the empty glass on the counter, he walked down the steps, running his hands along the railing, contemplating the best way to invite her to a high-stakes game in the private room.

Meanwhile, that same couple joined her at the table. The older duo from the afternoon, and this time they were dressed in evening attire, if you could call it that. Matching polo shirts. He shook his head, but had to hand it to Julia Fucking Bell. She knew how to pick 'em, and she had a pair of perfect plants with her. He bet they had a criminal record too, just like that Tad Herman she'd met with earlier.

He ambled past the VIP room, tapping his knuckles against the wall, a reminder that he'd get her in there soon enough.

Then he'd find out all the things he needed to know. Every. Single. Thing.

CHAPTER TEN

Friday, 7:14 p.m., Las Vegas

The drive to Vegas was smooth sailing on the 15—not a wink of traffic and he managed the route at eighty-five miles an hour, blasting Tom Petty's *Greatest Hits*, one of the best road-trip albums ever. As he handed the keys to the valet at the Allegro, he checked his messages. Brent had texted that he'd snagged the gift and would keep it safely stowed until Clay needed it.

One less thing for him to worry about. The rocky start to the day was behind him, the stress over and done. The rest of the weekend he'd be fucking busy and busy fucking. That's what he told himself as he stabbed the up button for the elevator in the hotel. He needed to take a piss, wash his hands, and then get downstairs and gather up Julia. Once inside the elevator, he stretched his neck from side to side, trying to work out the kinks from the drive. He'd been tense the whole time, racing against the clock, tearing down the highway, eager to get the weekend back on track. Rubbing his hand against the back of his neck, he tried to work out the knots when the elevator dinged at the twenty-first floor.

Three minutes later, he was back in the lift, shooting down to the lobby level, ready to find Julia and his brother at the blackjack tables where Brent said they were playing and winning. Good. Julia deserved to win every damn hand this weekend, and then some.

As he made his way through the lobby and across the crowds, something shifted in the air. A chill ran through him and his skin tingled coldly with the unmistakable sensation of being watched. Looking behind him, he spotted a tall man in a dark suit. His blood froze. *Just like Julia had said.*

In seconds, the man was gone.

Clay shook his head, rubbed his eyes, and wondered if he was seeing things, or if there was something more to Julia's fears. Or if there was something more to Charlie being angry with him. Was he tracking them? Getting ready to pounce?

But then all worries were stripped from his brain when he found her at the blackjack table thirty feet away. *Wearing her pearls.* A bolt of heat tore through his body. The memory of that morning flashed before him like a film reel playing his favorite clips. Sliding the beads over her, watching her reaction as her eyes went hazy with desire. Her asking him to put them inside her, then him tugging them out as she leaned her head back, her mouth falling open, her shout ringing in his ears from her orgasm.

My God, she was stunning in every way.

He didn't take his eyes off her the whole time as he walked up to her. Hell, he couldn't *not* look at her—his smart, sassy, bold, confident, and fiery woman. She was made for him; he was made for her. Never had two people been so perfectly matched. Everyone else in the whole casino faded away, a sea of shadowy bodies in shades of gray, and she alone was in Technicolor to him. Her flames of hair, her emerald eyes, the creamy skin of her strong legs, the clingy black skirt, the sexy green top, and the silver bracelet on her wrist that slipped a few inches as she placed her two cards down, splitting her hand. She was all color to him, radiant, high-definition color, bright and beautiful. She was the only one he saw, the only one he ever wanted to see.

The sight of her turned the temperature in his body all the way up, reaching volcanic levels as he neared her. He swore he could smell her, the sexy-sweet scent of her neck, her hair, her body. He inhaled, and it wafted through him. Or maybe it was just his imagination because she was permanently ingrained in his senses, the imprint of her scent a homing device connecting them.

She didn't see him walking over to her, nor did Brent, so he could do his favorite thing.

Surprise her.

First, he gently fingered a strand of her hair, a soft curl at the ends. A fluttery, barely-there touch, but enough for her to tighten her shoulders, then turn to him. The second she saw him, her eyes lit up. They were sparkling with excitement. It had only been eight hours since he'd seen her, but it felt like weeks, and to be greeted like this was one of the very many reasons he intended to put a ring on her finger this weekend.

Moving quickly, he bent his head to her ear. "I know where those pearls have been, and it makes me so fucking hard to see them on you in public."

She shivered, then tugged him to her, angling his erection against her hip. "Is this for me?" she whispered in his ear, her voice like a shot of desire through his system, ratcheting him up another notch.

"All for you. Only for you. And I need you now."

She tossed her cards on the table. "I think this hand is a bust," she said to the dealer, but kept her eyes on Clay.

His brother stared at him with a knowing look on his face. "You dog," Brent said, grinning, like he knew what Clay was about to do.

Clay clapped him on his back, and gave him a big hug. "I've missed you. And I owe you big time. And we're going to see your show in twenty minutes and have a drink or two after. But right now—"

Brent cut him off, waving his hand. "I gotta go too. The stage beckons."

Minutes later they were in the elevator, and they weren't alone. Surrounded by other guests, Clay aligned his body with hers, her back to his front. She wriggled subtly, and he hissed under his breath. "Careful."

"Or what?" she tossed back.

When the elevator reached their floor, letting them out, he spun her around, her chest pressed to the wall, and pinned both of her wrists above her head. "Or this," he said, lining his body up against hers, and sliding his free hand up, up, up the inside of her leg until he reached her panties. "Or I will fuck you in the hall."

"You say that like I wouldn't want you to fuck me in the hall," she said.

"You say that like you wouldn't care about anyone seeing us," he said, rubbing his hard cock against her. Off in the distance, he was vaguely aware of another guest leaving a room and heading in their direction to the elevators.

"I wouldn't care, Clay. I just want you," she said. "Now, please can we finish what we started with the texts?"

He moved his hand from between her legs, up to her breasts, palming one delicious globe in his free hand. "You want me to fuck your breasts?"

"I do. I really do."

He dropped her wrists, grabbed a hand, and led her into their room a few doors down. The door was still closing as she stripped off her skirt, her shirt, her bra, her breasts tumbling free while he shucked off his clothes.

With only her red-soled heels on, she moved to the bed, and spread herself out on the royal-blue covers, then pressed her breasts together. "Come here," she said, huskily.

"That's a double entendre," he said playfully as he stalked over to her.

"I know. Now straddle me. Climb over me," she said, her eyes never leaving his as she started giving the orders. He didn't know it was possible to be more aroused than he had been a few moments ago. But it was possible, because he was aching. His dick throbbed, to the point of painful with the need to have her.

"Touch yourself first."

He kneeled over her, one leg on either side of her breasts. She'd put herself in a thoroughly submissive position and he was dominating her physically, but somehow she was in charge too.

He gripped his cock in one hand, and she wrapped her hand over his. She guided him, their hands together stroking him. "Now, bring your cock to my mouth. I need to get you all ready to fuck my breasts."

She pressed her head back against the pillow, her red hair spread out like a fan.

"You sure you can handle this? I don't have it in me to go easy right now. An entire day away from you on a fucking vacation is torture."

"I can always handle it," she said, guiding him to her lips. He grabbed the headboard as he straddled her face. His eyes floated shut the second her lips wrapped around him, tremors slamming into his body as her warm mouth gave him some temporary relief from all this wanting.

She took him all the way in, her tongue lapping him up, her mouth turning him on even more.

"You mouth should be illegal, it's so fucking good," he growled as he thrust into her throat.

A few more pumps, and then her hands were on his hips and she pushed him off. "Now give me what I want," she said, eyeing her breasts.

She pushed them together, and they looked even bigger, rounder, and more inviting as she created the perfect warm cave. He slid his cock between the soft flesh and began pumping.

"You've been wanting this all day?" he asked as the head of his dick hit her lips, and her tongue darted out, flicking the tip.

"Yes," she said as he continued moving on her.

"Why?"

"Because I want you every way, Clay. Because I love when you need to fuck me in different ways. And because right now, all I want is for you to get off."

His shoulders shuddered as he thrust, the lingering wetness from her tongue and the smooth, tight friction from her breasts caressing his hard-on. She was fucking perfect with the appetite to match his, and the desire to please too.

"God, you take good care of me, but I want you to come too."

"I know you do. But right now I want a gift like the one you gave me this morning. I want a different kind of pearl necklace. I want you all over me," she said, those lusty eyes of hers making it clear how badly she needed this. That was all it took. If she wanted this, he'd give it to her. Hell, he needed it. He needed the release. So he fucked her breasts relentlessly, and she swirled her tongue against the head of his cock with each thrust, until soon an unyielding climax began in the base of his spine, then traveled through his body.

"Come on me," she whispered, urging him on. "Come all over me."

So he did, marking her the way she wanted, and she lapped up what she could then spread the rest over her breasts, like a sexy, greedy, naughty woman who only had eyes for him.

And he for her.

He collapsed next to her, still panting hard.

"Be right back," she said, and headed to the bathroom to clean up. When she returned, she glanced at the time. "We need to go to your brother's show. We don't want to be late and it starts soon."

"I know," he said, flashing her a grin. "But come fuck my face. I can't go to the show without eating you first."

"Clay," she chided, narrowing her eyes as she parked her hands on her hips. She was naked, but for her black heels that were truly fuck-me pumps.

"That's not helping me not want you," he said, making a circular motion as he gestured to her. "The whole full-naked look only makes me want you more."

"You are insatiable."

"So are you."

"I know, but still, we need to go."

"Then let me give you the two-minute treatment like you did to me in the car this morning," he said, patting the bed. "Come grind that sweet pussy on my face and let me feel you come on me."

She rolled her eyes, but seconds later she was straddling him, spreading her legs over his face. Her hands gripped the headboard as she lowered herself. "Ride me," he whispered hotly, the last words to come out of his mouth before his senses were assaulted by the decadent and delicious taste of her arousal flooding his tongue, his lips, his mouth. He licked her and kissed her, sucking hard with his mouth while flicking his tongue against her swollen clit. This wouldn't take long at all. He could tell by her taste, by how wet she was, by the way she humped his face as he grabbed hold of her hips and helped her rock against him at a frantic pace. Her moans grew louder, higher, needier, and soon he felt her pussy twitch, her thighs tighten, and her body shudder against him, the taste of her pleasure flowing over his tongue as he drank her in. Another soft kiss of her pussy, his lips savoring all of her. A gentle press, brushing his mouth against her center. Then a barely-there, goodbye kiss. He'd be back here soon, though. Very, very soon.

Then he smacked her ass, shifted her off him, and said in a teasing tone, "Woman, you're taking too long. We need to go."

"You're lucky I love you and let you talk to me that way," she said, with a wink.

"I am lucky that you love me. I am the luckiest son-of-a-bitch."

He didn't need that tie. He had her.

CHAPTER ELEVEN

Friday, 10:08 p.m., Las Vegas

He watched her walk away in the club, zigzagging through the slew of half-drunk, mostly-wasted, and completely-trashed patrons at Brent's club.

Finally, he lost sight of her long red locks as she turned the corner to the restrooms.

When he shifted his attention back to Brent, his brother was staring hard at him as if to say *what gives.*

"What?"

"What am I? Chopped liver?"

"Compared to her? More like chopped liverwurst," Clay teased, then took a drink of his scotch. He was in the not-quite-drunk-but-most-definitely-half-buzzed category. Brent was steely-eyed sober, and had one more show tonight. He'd finished his eight p.m. set before a raucous crowd that had rewarded him with the one thing a comedian craves more than anything—uncontrollable laugher. A woman in the back of the club had laughed so loudly during his routine on how hard it is to shave your own balls that she'd snorted, then shouted that she planned to toss her panties on stage at the end of the show.

She'd been mostly drunk, and had wound up keeping her clothes on, but had indeed rushed the stage after, trying to give him her number. Now, the stage was clear and "Luck Be a Lady" by Frank Sinatra piped through the club's sound system before Brent's late-night set kicked off soon.

"Maybe I won't relinquish that ring to you then."

Clay clapped him on the back. Hard. "Yeah. I'm not even going to acknowledge you said that."

"But yet you just did."

"So, how's the ring?"

Brent clasped his fingers together and fluttered his eyelashes, somehow managing to rearrange his features to look like a simpering Disney cartoon character. "Oh, it's just so, so pretty," he said in an affected tone.

Clay rolled his eyes. "Seriously. We're all set for tomorrow, night?"

Brent took a drink of his Diet Coke and nodded. Both men were serious now. Clay's brother might be a jokester, but he knew that his role as wingman in this proposal plan was not be toyed with. "Everything is in place. Think she'll say yes?"

Clay had complete and utter confidence in their love, but it was never a love to take for granted. Nor was a yes. He'd already made assumptions once and had nearly lost her. There would be no presumptions of a yes; only a great hope for one. "I hope so," he answered plainly.

Brent smiled. "She'll say yes."

"Thanks again for taking care of the package today. I'll get that tomorrow too. And I got your text that all was well, but also wanted to ask, did you talk to your friend in more detail about security? Are they watching Julia?"

"I did talk to her after Julia left with you. Mindy said there's no special attention being paid to her. All the hotels had beefed up security after a string of robberies a few months ago at some casinos off the Strip. Can't be too safe, she said. They thought it was mob-related. Michael Lawson is the Tony Soprano of this town; he runs a few rackets here in Vegas, but no one ever found a connection to the robberies. Besides, that's not Lawson's style—stealing chips. Anyway, a few were solved, but now they're thinking the thieves are just thieves, plain and simple, and they've spread out into a small pick-pocket ring, lifting chips here and there. Dealers are coming up short at the end of the night. That's making the casinos more concerned in general, and some are even offering rewards for information leading to apprehension," Brent said, and the extra men in suits thronging the hotel premises now made sense. Casinos were always going to be targets for brazen robbers, but robbers were not mobsters. They went after money, not people, so he could breathe a little easier.

"Should I be concerned about a pickpocket ring?" Clay joked. Because *pickpockets?* That was small potatoes and hardly anything to worry about. Hell, New York City was teeming with them. You keep your eyes open, you don't leave your wallet in your back pocket on the subway, and you don't nod off on public transit. Simple as that. Pickpockets were not a cause for his concern. They weren't on the same level as Charlie. Not even in the same solar system.

"Yeah, keep your chips close to you," Brent said, but then turned serious. "But, I gotta ask. Why would you be so concerned?"

Clay's chest tightened. He and Julia were done with her debt and the trouble was behind her, so he didn't want to let on, or reveal her secrets. But he'd been asking his brother to run intel, so he had to give him something. "She had some trouble with her ex. He left her with a steaming heap of problems, and they've been resolved, but I'm always on my guard."

Brent nodded several times, and that was all it took, all he needed to tell him. "I hear ya. But nothing to worry about it. It's all about the hotels trying to be pristine even when it comes to something as minor as lifting a few chips."

Clay noticed Julia in his peripheral vision, and soon she'd rejoined them. "So, boys, what'll it be? Are we staying for the next show?"

Brent wiggled his eyebrows, and pointed his thumb at Julia. "See? I like her. She's up for an encore of me."

Clay draped his arm around Julia. She raised her hand, linking her fingers through his. "We're taking off. I have plans for her."

"Plans?" she asked eagerly.

"Just you wait and see."

* * *

He studied his notes once more. The man bothered him; squeaky clean, he had the reputation of a choirboy in business. Nothing shady, nothing underhanded. Damn near impeachable on paper. He scrolled through the documents he'd researched on Clay Nichols that he'd stored in his phone since the man had arrived in town. Local family, varsity football, pre-law, then Yale law school, and ten years as an attorney. No debt, no trouble. He tucked his phone in his pocket, annoyance rolling through him. Neither one had made a move yet, but he knew, he fucking knew she would any second. She was gone for the night, but he had his associate tailing her, and the two of them were at the Venetian.

He had eyes everywhere so if she started hustling there, he'd be ready. He protected the Venetian too. For now, he threaded his way through the $100 tables, and found the couple she'd been hanging with earlier.

Time to make their acquaintance.

Then a bird trilled softly in his ear, and he straightened his spine, recognizing the ringtone. He snagged the phone from his pocket to double check that it was coming from a 415 area code. It was, so he did a 180, turning away from the tables. His contact was ringing him.

"I thought we had a deal," he said as he answered the call from San Francisco.

"We did."

CHAPTER TWELVE

Friday, 11:52 p.m., Las Vegas

The music was indistinguishable. She had no clue as to the words, or if there even were lyrics. But the song didn't need them. This was music that was *felt*, that thrummed through her body, that made her feel like a guitar being played.

The low bass, the rhythmic beat, and the sexy voice of the singer all did what they were supposed to do—put you in the mood to dance horizontally. Soon, she'd be doing just that. For now, she was still vertical and moving to the beat at Tao, a nightclub at the Venetian.

It was a Friday night in Vegas, and the posh club was teeming with hot, young, sweaty things wrapped up in each other. Neon-blue lights illuminated the bar, manned by fit and pretty bartenders, concocting pink, blue and orange drinks, and pouring the occasional vodka or scotch, like the ones they'd ordered and downed. Now, she was swaying her hips to the techno beat, grinding against Clay. Because that's what you do at a nightclub. You bump. You grind. You simulate all the naughty things you want to do later. Well, maybe not *all*. But enough of those things, and right now her body was nearly plastered to his, her arm raised and wrapped around his neck, his hand holding tightly to her hip. She rubbed against him, and he pulled her close to his pelvis. Their constant need to touch each other, to find ways to get closer, to erase all the negative space between them was thick in the air. She stretched her neck against his shoulder, leaning back to look at him.

"What would Tad Herman say if he saw us now?"

"I don't know. Is public copulation forbidden in your morals clause?" he whispered in her ear.

"I'm not sure. Are you planning on copulating with me here on the dance floor?"

"Here. There. Everywhere. But only if it's legal."

"The things you to do my body are clearly illegal, so I think we've already violated all the clauses."

"Gorgeous, there are so many more ways I want to violate you. I'll never stop wanting to infringe on morals when it comes to your sinful body," he said, then licked a path from her collarbone, up to her ear, and she purred, her arousal ratcheting higher.

She pointed to the bar. "Go over there. Pretend you're a stranger."

"I'll see if I can find the hottest woman here."

"You do that."

He let go of her and walked away. He leaned against the bar, scanning the club, ably playing the part of a single man cruising for chicks. She watched him as his eyes drifted across the sea of bodies, writhing and twisting, tangling and untangling, then landed on hers.

They locked eyes, and she kept her gaze fixed on him as she danced alone. She ran a hand through her hair, then shook out her red strands around her face. Moving her right hand to her breasts, she let it travel through her cleavage, down her belly, and then to the top of her skirt. She danced, a sexy, subtle dance for him and her fingers splayed across her stomach, the tips of them precariously close to dipping under her skirt. He never stopped watching her, and she thrilled at his reaction, at the way his eyes were only on her, at the lusty look in them. He stalked across the dance floor, and yanked her against him.

"Hey stranger, I'm thinking pretty seriously about taking you to that dark alcove in the corner, and showing you what I can do with my hands." He tipped his forehead to the corner of the club where tall windows looked out on the terrace, home to more dancing, drinking, and sweating. Each window was framed by an arch, giving the tiniest bit of privacy if you wedged yourself in just right.

"Show me," she said, and let him guide her to the farthest one.

He boxed her in, resuming their position from the dance floor. The lower half of her body was hidden by the wall below the window, the upper half visible against the glass to anyone on the balcony who cared to look at the lovers pretending to be strangers. He rubbed his erection against her rear, then slipped his hand around her waist, his fingers inching under her blouse, spreading over her belly. She drew a sharp breath. "Since I've never touched you before, I'm not sure how you like it. I'm going to have to try different things."

"I'm all for experimentation," she said as he traced soft, lazy lines over her belly, knowing full well that she loved it when he touched her stomach.

"What about this then?" he said, drawing a path up to her breasts. "Is there any chance you like having your breasts touched?"

"As a matter of fact, I like it when my man fucks them."

He growled in her ear and slammed his hips against her. "And what about this?" He dipped his fingers into the waistband of her skirt, tapping them against her underwear. "I don't suppose you're a fan of manual stimulation?"

"I'm quite fond of it, as a matter of fact. I did it to myself this afternoon."

He inhaled sharply, breathing hard against her neck, his arms tightening around her. He'd be reaching that point she craved soon, all heat and tension and palpable need for her. She loved that he was like this. That he still wanted her as much today as he had the night they'd met. "Will you still want me this much in a year?" she whispered, letting go of their play.

"I thought we were strangers," he said.

She shook her head, shedding the role-play. "I don't want to be strangers with you."

"Good. Because I don't either. I want to be the man who knows you," he said, his voice gentle, his touch tender as he brushed his lips against her neck.

"I like it better like this," she said, letting him hear the vulnerability in her voice, in her heart. "I love that you know me. I love that you know my body, and my heart, and my mind."

"I love knowing you, Julia," he said, cupping her cheek and turning her face so he could look her in the eyes. "I love that we're not strangers. That we're not uncertain. That we're not on opposite coasts anymore."

"That we're together," she added, flashing him a smile that wasn't sexy or naughty or wicked. That was simply *true,* like all she felt for him.

"Always," he added. "I want to be the man who loves you always."

"I want to be loved by you always," she said, and her heart skipped ten thousand beats. They were treading near the territory that she desperately wanted. She'd hoped so hard that he'd propose this weekend, and while she knew he wasn't about to get down on one knee in a nightclub, her heart filled with joy at how he promised— *so easily*—to love her always. He brushed a thumb over her lips, and she swore she could see forever in his eyes.

"You will be," he whispered, and she knew that he meant every word, that he would love her like this— deeply, passionately, truly—for their whole lives. He closed his eyes and fused his mouth to hers in a slow kiss that turned her knees to jelly. Equal parts desire and love surged through her as her stomach flipped wildly.

He took his time kissing her, his lips lingering on hers, savoring her mouth, lapping at her tongue. She moaned softly, and he broke the kiss. "Always," he added. He ran his hand down the fabric of her blouse and she shivered against him.

"God, you make me feel so good. Everything you do turns me on, Clay. When you tell me you want to fuck me it turns me on, and when you tell me you love me, it turns me on," she said as the loud music pulsed around them, and club-goers danced on the balcony. But the lights were dim, the corner was dark, and he was all that mattered to her.

"I love you and I want to fuck you," he said as his fin-gers skipped past her belly and down the front of her skirt.

"Mmmm," she murmured, a thrill racing through her, and turning into heat between her legs. "Like that. That turned me on."

"Let me check," he said, slinking his hand up the in-side of her thigh, and flicking it once against the cotton panel of her panties.

"Oh God," she gasped even as he took his touch away.

"You love being touched, don't you," he said, and it wasn't a question. It was the full truth.

"By you. Touch me more, please," she said, her voice shaky with want. She felt like she'd disintegrate if he didn't touch her right now.

"I will, but I don't want anyone seeing you getting so aroused, so you need to stay here and keep your eyes on the balcony. My body will hide you," he told her, as he kept her caged in with his broad chest, strong arms, and his height, like a protective shield covering up her desire, keeping it in a precious cocoon. Even though they were in public, surrounded by drinkers and dancers, she felt like they were all alone: the two of them, shrouded in the way they felt.

His fingers returned to her panties, and this time he slid them down the front of her underwear, his finger brushing over her clit.

"I want to tell you all the things I love about your pussy, Julia," he whispered hotly as he stroked her clit, his other hand keeping a firm grip on her hip.

"Tell me," she said, her voice so desperate, her need for him so unbelievably high. She felt as if she might combust, rocket on out of here from the way he stroked her. Masterfully. This was no stranger's touch. This was a lover's touch. The touch of a man who knew, who had studied, who'd listened, who'd taken his time and learned everything that pleased his woman and then some.

"These are the things I love. How when I first slip my hand inside your panties I find that wet spot on the cotton panel that tells me you're hot for me," he said, sliding his fingers across her. "Like right now, and then when I first touch your pussy, you're already wet all over, with my favorite lubricant—your desire." She shut her eyes, and was starting to see stars. She began to rock gently against his hand, and he let her. He didn't try to stop her movements because she kept them subtle enough. "And you're so sleek and soft on the outside, and hot on the inside," he said, sliding a finger inside to demonstrate. She hitched in a breath as he continued his ode to her pussy. "And your panties get so wet they're useless."

Another gasp. Another sharp inhale. A moan stifled in her throat.

"I love that I do this to you," he said, circling her clit faster with the pad of his thumb, thrusting his index finger in and out. "That you're wetter now than the night I met you, that I can still whisper in your ear, and tell you all the things I want to do to your sweet, delicious, perfect pussy and it still makes you quiver in my arms," he said against her neck, layering a hard kiss on her skin as he continued lavishing attention between her legs. "And I love that as I move my fingers, and slide them over you and in you, and on that fucking fantastic clit, I can feel your wetness all over my hand."

Her belly tightened, and the walls inside her felt like they were about to come tumbling down. She grew wetter, hotter, and she could feel her arousal dampen his hand. She bit back a cry.

"Just like that. I can feel more of you right now, Julia. I love that as you get more and more turned on, it feels like you're gushing on me."

"I am," she whispered breathily, the whole world behind her eyelids like hot flashing light as pulses of pleasure spread through her body.

"When I watch you touch yourself, I can literally see your desire for me," he said, his finger plunging deeper, his thumb swirling faster against her aching, throbbing clit. "And when I bury my face between your legs, I feel like I'm drinking you, and I can't get enough."

Involuntarily, she started rocking into his hand, and panting—panting so fucking hard as her orgasm took hold, and she desperately wanted to shout. She pressed her teeth into her bottom lip, and immediately he clasped his hand over her mouth. "Cry out in my hand. I'm the only one who can hear you," he said in her ear, the music in the club keeping their secret.

She moaned against his palm, his hand silencing her screams of bliss as he stroked the last few waves of her climax from her, his fingers inside her and outside her, sending her far into the beautiful abyss of pleasure and love.

Eventually, when her body stopped shuddering, he smoothed out her skirt and blouse and licked her taste off his fingers. "Do you think we just violated your morals clause?"

She laughed. "If anyone saw us, surely we broke all the rules of decorum."

"If anyone is looking, I hope they're jealous as fuck because I get to have the most fantastic woman in the world."

* * *

Back at the hotel a little later, he gave her another present wrapped in shiny paper. When she opened it, she ran her fingers over the silver metal of the handcuffs, inscribed with the name of the manufacturer, Joy Delivered, a high-end maker of sex toys.

Then he cuffed her, held her wrists behind her back in one hand, grabbed hold of her hair in the other and delivered more joy to her as he took her bent over the bed, the only man who would ever make her feel this way, the only man who would could fuck her when she was on all fours and still make her feel like a queen.

But she did. She felt like queen of the world, ruler of the heavens and earth *even* with her ass in the air, her hair pulled tight, her hands shackled. In that pose—that bound pose of submission— he sent her soaring, owning her body, because he wanted her to feel extraordinary. She did, oh God, she did as he pleased her, over and over and over.

* * *

Judging from the report of his associate, there'd been no card hustling going on tonight with those two, just a whole lot of public near-fornication at Tao. His dick twitched angrily as he thought of that man having his hands all over that luscious redhead. She was a hot little thing, and it pissed him off that he was horny for her.

It made him want to get to the bottom of this even faster. Get her out of his way. She was a target, nothing more.

Besides, a deal was a deal was a deal, and the fact that she was here, sniffing around his turf, made it clear that terms had been broken. She was the evidence of clauses not being followed.

On his way out of the Allegro he spotted the guy she'd been having drinks with at the pool earlier. At least, it looked like him from the picture he'd seen: young face, skinny build, the guy with the hoodie again. He was playing the slots right now, trying to ring up some money from Dolly Parton. Hmmm. He looked like a regular old casino tourist, and he wasn't sure what to make of him, or how the guy was connected to Julia.

He went home that night, determined to handle her tomorrow. He couldn't risk fucking up this gig; the last one had been botched, and this was his chance to make good. Once inside his home, he dug through a carton of leftovers in the fridge, hunting for something to eat before bed. But what he found was a week old, maybe more, judging from the smell. He tossed the rancid carton in the trash and went to bed hungry, mad as hell and ready for tomorrow.

CHAPTER THIRTEEN

Saturday, 11:14 a.m., Las Vegas

After a breakfast of scrambled eggs, toast and home fries, Clay took another swallow of his coffee, finishing the cup. They sat at the breakfast table by the window of their hotel suite, him in his boxer briefs, her in a cami and lacy underwear. If he hadn't just enjoyed two rounds of morning sex—one in bed, one in the shower—he'd have ripped off the panties. But he was sated.

For now.

Julia chewed the last bite of her toast, then checked her phone. She'd been antsy to hear from Tad after the meeting yesterday when he dispensed his be-a-good-girl rules. Clay was eager too to get a look-see at the morals clause. Strange item for a liquor company, but he could also see how stipulations like that might be necessary. A beverage-maker wouldn't want a drunk representing its drinks. In fact, such clauses might even be more vital for a product that loosened lips and relaxed judgment.

She tapped the screen. "I knew it. Saturday morning and he's already all over me. Here's a note from Tad, and he wants to know if I received the contract addendum and if I plan on signing it."

He motioned with his fingers for her to hand him the phone. "Let me see those documents."

She clicked open the PDF in her email and handed it to Clay. He took a minute to read it over. When he set down the phone, he simply said, "Hmm."

"Hmmm what?"

"This hardly seems necessary. Which makes me think it's personal."

Julia pointed to herself. "Personal about me?"

"Or him."

"In what way?"

"It might be a hot-button issue for him. Let's see what we can find out."

"You figured that all out from looking at a one-page contract addendum?" she asked, arching an eyebrow.

He nodded. "Call it a gut feeling. Everyone has a motive. When someone is pushing hard for something in business it's almost always personal. Take Gino at Comedy Nation. His wife just left him. Messy divorce, and she's taking him to the cleaners. His negotiation style goes from hard-ass to complete prick. Now this Tad guy?

I don't know him from Adam, but I'll bet you the keys to the handcuffs that something is up."

She reached out a hand to shake. "I'm not doubting you. I'm only shaking because I have a thing for handcuffs."

He grinned, and stretched across the table to give her a quick kiss. Then he lobbed in a call to his friend Cam, and asked him to run intel on Tad.

As he hung up the call, he steeled himself for what might be a tough topic—Charlie, and the way things had ended with him yesterday. Pissing off a gangster was, generally speaking, not a good idea, and Charlie Stravinsky was most decidedly mad at him.

"Julia," he started, clearing his throat. "You know how we made a promise to always be open? No more secrets?"

"Of course," she said, shooting him a quizzical look. Small lines of tension knitted across her brow.

"I called Charlie yesterday," he said, then shared the details of the call, down to the cold end of it when Charlie had hung up, pissed.

"Shit," she said, sucking in a breath. "That's not good."

"I know. But I actually think it's not going to be too hard to make good with him."

"A man like Charlie is a man no one needs on their bad side."

"And I've got a few ideas I'm mulling about."

"You're not going to go into business with him, are you?" she asked, her eyebrows now shooting up to her hairline.

He laughed deeply, and shook his head. "No. You know me—I've built my law firm on the backbone of being squeaky clean and it's served me well. Just a little something to say I'm sorry is all I'm thinking."

"You gotta be careful, Clay," she said, her voice now intensely serious, her eyes flashing him some kind of warning. She held up her hands, turning them into claws. "When he gets his hooks in you, he doesn't let go until he gets every last bite. He's like a lion chasing down a gazelle."

"I don't know how to tell you this, so let's just cut to the chase. I know how to be a lion too."

She tilted her head. "I know you do. Though I see you as more of a tiger. You're my tiger," she said, then purred playfully. "But be careful. Especially now."

"Especially with Tad expecting you to only consort with upstanding people."

"I'll admit it; I do kind of want the expanded deal. Being a spokesperson for my drink? I like the idea. I'm proud of that drink, and what it's done for me, how it launched my career to a new level."

"As you should be. So don't worry. I won't get close to a gangster and sully your squeaky-clean reputation anywhere but in the bedroom."

"And that's where I'm anything but squeaky clean," she said, and stood up from her chair, walked the few feet over to him and sat down in his lap. "Dirty me up again, you sexy thing."

"Gladly."

* * *

He glanced out the hotel window as Julia blow-dried her hair. The sun was rising high; it was a little past noon. He planned to pop the question in the afternoon because she'd least suspect that. A fancy dinner out at the Paris hotel? A late night-proposal in a gondola at the Venetian? That's precisely what she'd expect. But he'd surprise her if he asked her in the middle of the day. Catch her off-guard, ask the question, make her melt.

He hoped.

He never wanted to take anything for granted, not in business and not in love, and certainly never with Julia. But damn, he'd pictured it, scripted it, and imagined her response. He hoped to hell she wanted this as much as he did. A forever together.

Snagging his phone from the table, he tapped out a quick text to Brent. *Ten minutes.*

His reply arrived seconds later. *Ten-four.*

He deleted the trail of evidence—the thread of messages between himself and his brother this morning. Not that Julia would ever go snooping, but he didn't want one to accidentally pop up.

A few minutes later, she'd clicked off the dryer, so he headed to the bathroom and stood in the door. "I heard from Cam. Want to know what Tad's story is?"

She nodded eagerly, her green eyes lighting up as she fluffed out her hair with her fingers. "Tell me. And make it tawdry, please. I want to know that he was a very bad boy, that he likes spankings from nuns, and that he covers it all up by acting like a goody-goody two shoes."

He tapped his finger on his nose and pointed at her. "Bingo."

"Really?"

"Pretty much. Cam did a check on him. He goes to church every Sunday. He volunteers at the local homeless shelter. And he has a prior for—get this—" Clay stopped to pause because it was funny as hell "—shoplifting."

She rolled her eyes and laughed as she spread lotion on her legs, fabulously on display in sexy black shorts. "Are you kidding me?"

He held up his hands. "I kid you not. Cam just sent me the details. Happened when Tad was in college in Florida."

"Let me guess. He was lifting an Almond Joy from the local supermarket?"

"Nope. It's better than that. Brace yourself," he said, leaning against the door as she looped the cord around the hairdryer. "The man stole a bottle of Bacardi from the liquor store."

She burst out laughing. "Oh, that's fabulous. He steals rum and then goes on to work for a liquor company. How did that get past HR at Farrell?"

"I'm going out on a limb here, but I'm guessing there are no background checks when your daddy works for the company."

Laughter continued to ring through the hotel suite. But then, just as quickly as it had started, it stopped. Julia's face turned serious as she reached for her watch, sliding it onto her wrist like an elastic bracelet. She'd always said she hated watches that fastened like belts, or required loops and clasps. Funny, how a person who didn't mind being restrained in bed had such strong opinions on other kinds of restraints. "Wait," she said. "Maybe I shouldn't be laughing. Maybe he really is this good, upstanding guy now. Reformed and all. It's possible, right?"

He nodded. "Of course. It's entirely possible. Or it's entirely possible that he's the morals police because he has something to hide. Either way, I'll talk to him on Monday. But I don't think it's a problem to sign the addendum anyway. It's about future behavior. It's not some retroactive clause, so they don't have a say over your past connections with Charlie. It's all about the future."

"Let's just hope those guys I thought were tailing me aren't working for Charlie then. I don't want to be suspected by association," she said, as she grabbed a small tin of lip balm from her makeup case, then swiped some of it on her lips before dropping the tin into her back pocket of her linen shorts.

"They're not following you. It's just hotel security. Brent checked for me."

"All right, are you ready to go play some poker? Because I've been jonesing to play with you all week," she said, reaching for his shirt collar and tapping her fingers against it. "Let's hit the tables and win some money."

"Let's go," he said, gesturing to the door when his phone rang.

Unknown number.

He pumped a mental fist at Brent's ability to go covert. Then, he did his best acting. Let his shoulders sag slightly. Turned his mouth into a hard, frustrated frown.

"Damn. It's Gino. From Comedy Nation," he said to Julia, then gestured to the phone. "I gotta take this." He answered. "Clay Nichols here."

Brent adopted his best asshole TV executive voice. "Hey dickhead. We gotta talk about this piece-of-shit contract. I had my cat pee on it this weekend because that's what it's worth to me."

Clay did everything to keep a straight face. "Hold on one second," he said, then placed his hand over the phone. "Go downstairs and play a few hands, okay? This'll take me fifteen minutes. Twenty, tops. But I need to get it ironed out. I promise I'll be there soon."

"Of course," she said, planting a quick kiss on his cheek, then grabbing her clutch purse from the foyer table, and waving a sexy goodbye. "See you in twenty minutes."

"Text me. Let me know where to find you," he whispered.

She blew him a kiss and mouthed *I will*, and he followed her to the door, holding it open, and planting a quiet kiss on her lips. He waved goodbye as she walked down the hall and pressed the down button for the elevator.

Once the door shut, he returned to his brother. "Okay, where are you?"

"On the twentieth floor. Stairwell. I have the ring and the necklace."

"Come up in two minutes. She's getting in the elevator right now."

Soon, his brother was in the room with him and Clay

set his eyes on the ring he was going to put on Julia's finger any minute. The damn thing near blinded him it was so bright.

Perfect. He slid it into his pocket, along with the necklace.

CHAPTER FOURTEEN

Saturday, 1:12 p.m., Las Vegas

She was feeling lucky today. But she wasn't going to base her decision on which table to choose on something as capricious as that.

Luck was here one minute, gone the next. A snap of the fingers, a wink of the eye, and luck drained faster than an iPhone battery. She had more than luck on her side. She had smarts, freedom, and most of all confidence, and she planned to use that full suite of tools as she tackled the tables. Weaving her way through the rattling of the roulette balls and the rolling of the craps dice, she fixed her eyes on the pai gow table ahead, and beyond that on the $100 minimum land. She'd had a good summer at Speakeasy, and her checks had been cashing quite nicely from the Purple Snow Globe award and drink contract, so she could afford this little luxury—a Saturday afternoon round or two at the Allegro.

At the pai gow table, a tall and terribly blond man walked behind the players, moving closer than someone usually does, and Julia narrowed her eyes, as if she could read him from several feet away. Something about him felt oddly familiar, even though she couldn't see his face. It was the shape of his shoulders, the straw shade of his hair. Some kind of gumshoe instinct flared deep in her, and she picked up her pace, walking fast across the carpet in her heels. He slipped past the gamblers, lifting his right arm a few inches then back down. She caught his profile, and instantly a name touched down on her tongue. She was very nearly sure who he was . . . but then he turned more, his large nose coming into view. As he moved, he reminded her of an eel slinking through the marshes unseen. No one noticed him, but when he turned away from the table, she zeroed in on his hand as he slid something into his pocket. She wouldn't want to finger-point in a court of law, but as a betting woman, she was willing to lay many chips down on the chance that he'd just pocketed a few that weren't his own.

She tried to follow him, race-walking past the dealer, around a beam, then down an aisle between the tables, but in seconds he was gone, probably lost in the crowd at the casino.

Damn. She nearly stomped her foot. But then, what would she have done if she'd caught up to him? "Excuse me, is that a handful of chips in your pocket, or are you just happy to scc me?"

Enough of her detective daydreams. Time to win some money for the hell of it.

She glanced at her watch. One-fifteen. Clay would be here in fifteen more minutes. She double backed to her destination. Settling in on a high-backed stool, she texted Clay her whereabouts, collected her chips and began placing her bets. Ten minutes later, she was $1000 richer.

God, she loved Vegas.

"Excuse me, you must be the very lovely Julia Bell."

The voice was smooth and honeyed—like a velvet lounge singer she could listen to all night. She turned to the face behind the voice and if she weren't madly in love with someone else, she might have found the man attractive. Magnetic amber eyes, a crooner's voice, and a tall, athletic build, with Jon Hamm-esque hair, wavy and gelled.

"Yes," she said, resisting the urge to roll her eyes at his line. But then, she was practiced at this kind of resistance having grown accustomed to a wide assortment of come-on lines at her bar. "What can I do for you, Don Draper?"

She couldn't help it. He had the whole *Mad Men* five-o-clock shadow thing working in spades, right down to the suit.

He shot her a smile, showing off nice, white teeth. "I am Dominic Stevenson, the floor manager here at the Allegro. I was sent here by a gentleman named Clay Nichols. He has arranged a special game for you in the VIP room. Would you do me the favor of allowing me to escort you to him?" The man held out his arm, crooking his elbow for Julia, like an escort at a debutante ball, ready to guide a young woman down the stairs to present her.

She could barely contain her smile. She couldn't help it. She was damn near grinning like a fool. This was the moment she'd been holding her breath for. He'd planned it perfectly like she knew he would, and had taken her by surprise. She'd never expected he'd pick a Saturday afternoon, and yet this was pure Clay. He'd wanted to give her back her love of poker with this trip, and for him to do it with such a grand gesture made her heart pound with joy for him. Everything added up, him sending her ahead, then setting this up for her. She didn't want to take this moment for granted, so she reminded herself to savor every second. She catalogued everything—the way her veins rushed fast with hope, the way the hair on her arms rose with goosebumps, the excitement that thrummed loudly through her bones like a vibration as she stood up from the table and took the gentleman's arm. She was eager, so very eager to see what her man had in store for her.

It all made sense—wonderful, blissful, gorgeous, sexy sense—that he'd somehow concocted a way to get down on one knee in the VIP poker room. She couldn't wait to say yes.

"Is he there now?" she asked Dominic.

"Yes. Ready for you," he said. They rounded the corner and entered the private room. He gripped her arm harder and dug his fingers in. The edges of her watch scraped roughly against her wrist. She tried to pull her arm away, but his hand was now a steel vise, and he wouldn't let go.

"Excuse me," she said, trying to wriggle out of his grip as they walked past an oval table and rich brown chairs, with opulent mirrors strategically angled to hide hands. "That's a bit too rough. Can you let up?"

"Not a chance in hell," he said, and his voice was no longer honey. It was malice.

Like a painful injection, all her excitement was erased, replaced by ice-cold fear coursing through her body as he clasped his hand over mouth, and shoved her hard through a doorway.

Then locked the door.

CHAPTER FIFTEEN

Saturday, 1:34 p.m., Las Vegas

The $100 table with the dealer with cropped black hair and one diamond earring.

He read the text from her one more time, studying the message as if it would reveal a clue as to where she could possibly be.

But there were only five $100 tables and he'd circled them fifty times each, looking for her. She was nowhere to be seen. He desperately wanted to believe he'd simply missed her.

He returned to the table she was supposed to be at. The dealer nodded at him this time as he dealt to four players. It was an I-see-you-look, an I'm-memorizing-your-face look. Clay nodded back, and paced more, his eyes roaming the casino, scanning the tables, checking out the nooks and crannies, the bars, the lounge chairs. He paced like a caged lion. He was sure he'd have security swarming him any second because he looked suspicious as hell. Checking his watch. Checking his phone. Running his hand roughly through his hair. Dialing, over and over.

He spun around in another circle, hunting for signs for the nearest ladies room. Hell, maybe she was taking a piss. A long fucking piss. He marched over to the sign, and waited twenty seconds until a woman with dark hair, kind eyes and laugh lines made a beeline for the restroom.

"Excuse me. I'm looking for my–" he paused for a split second, the words catching in his throat because he was about to say *wife* when he stopped himself. "–my date, and I was supposed to meet her ten minutes ago. Would you mind asking if there's a Julia in the bathroom? Redhead, wearing black shorts and heels."

"Sure," the woman said, but she gave him a look as if he were crazy to ask, pathetic maybe. A pathetic guy who'd been stood up. Maybe he was. Hell, he sounded like a desperate man who'd been ditched by a woman. But he knew that wasn't the case.

He waited and called her again. Five rings then voicemail. Maybe she'd turned it on vibrate during the game. Maybe she'd even turned down the volume, figuring that was proper poker behavior or something.

But then, where was she? He held out hope that nature had called. That maybe she'd taken a long restroom trip.

A minute later, the dark-haired woman with laugh lines emerged, patted him on the arm, and shook her head ruefully. "Sorry, hon. No one was in there. I hope you find your lady. And if she's run out on you, you come find me and I'll be happy to be your date," she said, then winked at him and headed off.

"Thanks," he muttered, and shook his head at her proposition.

He could case the joint for all the ladies rooms, but instead he marched right back to the table with the diamond-earringed dealer. After he laid the last card down, Clay cleared his throat, and said, "Excuse me."

The dealer looked at him, his face impassive. "Yes?"

"Was there a redhead here a few minutes ago?" he asked then gave a quick description of Julia.

The dealer nodded.

"Any idea when she left? Where she went?"

"Played a few hands. Took off a few minutes ago," he said, his voice even, unreadable. Clay suspected dealers in Vegas were trained to reveal nothing—not while dealing, not while playing, and not when asked questions by patrons. Maybe even especially when asked by patrons.

"Did she happen to say where she was going?" he pressed.

"C'mon, man," said one of the guys at the table. "She's not here. Leave him alone so we can play."

Clay shot him a dirty look; a young, fratty guy who he wanted to punch for no rightful reason except that he was pissed, and worried, and starting to panic. He walked away from the table, looking for clues anywhere. He wanted the simple answer. The I-got-stuck-in-the-elevator answer. But as the minutes ticked by, those easy answers felt less likely. Unease deepened in his chest, spreading quickly like laundry soap overflowing from a washing machine.

His mind raced in rewind over the last twenty-four hours—her worries about being followed, the men in the suits, the pilot and the trouble with the plane, his own sense of being watched last night, and most of all—Charlie. Angry, pissed-off, mad-as-hell Charlie.

The dread in Clay grew roots, clawing through his organs, tearing up his insides like twisting, deadly weeds.

He prayed for that simple answer, the I-had-to-take-an-unexpected-call-from-my-sister-and-I'm-so-sorry-it-worried-you answer. But deep down, he knew something had gone wrong. Terribly wrong.

Grabbing his phone, he started to dial Brent to ask to be put in touch with hotel security when Julia's name flashed across his screen.

He released ten thousand breaths and answered in a nanosecond.

"Are you okay? Where are you?" he asked, not bothering to mask the worry.

But it wasn't Julia who was calling.

* * *

"How long have you been hustling here on my turf, Julia Bell? Just this weekend? Or have you been here longer?"

She sneered at him. "I'm not hustling."

He smacked her shoulder. Not too hard, more like the swat a kid brother gave his sister, but still, she didn't like it. Not one bit. They were in a small office behind the fancy VIP room, but it felt more like an interrogation cell given the circumstances.

"Get your fucking hands off me," she snarled, calling on her best poker skills because she didn't want this man to smell her fear. That was all she had—faking it. Inside, she was quivering, but she'd been trained—unintentionally—by the best of them. Being Charlie Stravinsky's pawn had taught her to show no fear. Even if her entire being was coated in terror right now.

"Don't scream," he warned. "If you scream . . ."

She didn't know what he'd do, or what else he had at his disposal in this tiny room. He had cuffs though, because once he'd slammed the door, the smooth-talking man pushed her down hard on a chair, and locked one hand to the slats of it. With her other hand free, she wasn't at the terrified level yet. But she sure as hell wasn't a fan of his *bully cop* routine. Who was he, though? Who did he work for? He'd said he was the floor manager, but was that a ruse? All she knew was he was a loose cannon, so she didn't scream.

Yet.

"I'll take my hands off you when you get the hell out of town," he added.

"Don't you worry. I don't have any interest in staying," she hissed. "And if you keep me here any longer I will scream. Let me go."

He raised a hand, stopping sharply in the air, but making it clear he'd hit. She flinched deep inside, but on the outside she barely showed a twitch.

"I run the games in this town. Not him. And I want you out of the games."

She furrowed her brow, and pointed with her free hand to the door. "The casino games out there?"

"No," he said crisply, punctuating the word. "And put that hand down," he said, pointing to her rebel left hand. She listened. For now. "The ones where we get the real money."

"What the hell are you talking about?"

"I know who you are. You were Charlie's girl. You took down his guys."

Her body tightened. She said nothing. She wasn't going to admit to anything, and not because of that dumb morality clause from Tad. She was admitting to nothing because that had been her policy when it came to her past—it was hers and hers alone. She owned it, and she kept her trap shut about it.

"And Michael had a deal with him. This is Michael's town, and Michael runs the games, and when you show up it pisses him off."

She drew a sharp breath and rolled her eyes. She wasn't acting when she said, "I have no clue who you're talking about. I don't know a Michael."

He scoffed at her, spittle flying dangerously near her face. Wincing, she raised her free hand to wipe her cheek. The irony, the absolute irony of her being cuffed twice in twenty-four hours was not lost on her, but she wasn't laughing over it. Nope, even though she was only bound by one hand as he peppered her with questions, she was quaking in her bones. She didn't know how the hell she was going to claw her way out of this heap of trouble, or if he simply planned to let her go after he shook her down. She cycled through her options. The door was several feet away. If she just freed her hand, she could make a run for it, grab the handle and run like hell out of here. She tried to slide her wrist from the cuff somehow, twisting and turning her hand. Maybe she could find the ideal angle to slip out.

"Michael is the Charlie Stravinsky of this town. That clear things up for you, sugar?"

She couldn't hide her reaction anymore. She cringed, squeezing her eyes shut painfully. Memories of Charlie's capriciousness, his manhandling and his sheer and utter vindictiveness crashed into her, rolling over her in painful waves. How the hell had she wound up in the crosshairs of another Charlie? Or Vegas's Charlie? Did she have a *kick me* sign on her back?

Dominic pointed at her, and sneered knowingly. "Ah, so now everything rings a bell, doesn't it?"

He kneeled down in front of her, his hands gripping her thighs, his breath hot on her face.

"No," she said.

"Let me make it as plain as fucking day, princess," he said, his pretty amber eyes looking twisted. "You're on the fucking list. We know you work for him, and we don't like it. Michael runs the executive games here, and no one else. He has a deal with Charlie to stay the fuck out of his turf and vice versa, so when you show up it sends a message to us that Charlie's encroaching, and we don't like it. So let's see how much he likes it when his top ringer starts working for us, and when you work for us, then I will be more than happy to show you what you've been missing on all fronts," he said, grabbing his crotch as if it were an offering to her, then returning his hands to her thighs and digging in harder.

And that did it. That fucking did it. No fucking way was this scumbag manhandling her *and* hitting on her in the nastiest way. In an instant, she launched her high-heeled foot forward and kicked him hard as a hammer in the balls with her sharp black heels. She sent him reeling backwards as he clutched his family jewels, crying out like a wounded animal. She joined him in the noise department, screaming as loudly as she could.

But the scream didn't last long. Within two seconds, he had his slimy hand on her mouth, silencing her.

CHAPTER SIXTEEN

Saturday, 1:39 p.m., Las Vegas

"Hi. I'm sorry I'm not Julia, but I found this phone right outside the VIP room. Your number was the last one dialed, and it looks like you've been calling too," the man on the other end said, and Clay wasn't sure whether to kiss the phone or slam it into the wall.

He opted for neither. This was a clue and hopefully it would take him to her. "Where are you right now?"

"By the blackjack tables. I've got on a pink shirt. I walked past the VIP room, and the phone was on the ground with a ton of missed calls, so I grabbed it," the man said, and Clay turned around and ran to the roulette tables, taking long, fast strides. At one point, a waiter called out to him to slow down but he ignored him, quickly finding the pink-shirted man with Julia's cell phone.

"You found it by the VIP room?"

"Yes, poker room."

Clay clapped him on the arm, scanned the tables quickly for signs of a VIP room along the walls, then spotted an arched doorway not far away. He took off again, gripping her phone while calling Brent with his own. His brother answered immediately and Clay didn't wait a second.

"There's trouble at the Allegro. I need you here right away. I need you to call your friends in security. I think something's happened to Julia," he said, and Brent responded with, "On it, now."

He stopped quickly at the entrance, expecting to find throngs of players, high rollers engaged in big bets, maybe even some scummy dealer holding her hostage. Hell, he was prepared to stumble upon Charlie himself, looking like the cat who ate the canary, all cool and collected and ready to impose new terms of servitude. But the room was cruelly quiet—empty and eerie, as if it had been cleared out on purpose. Off in the far corner, he spotted a brown door that nearly blended into the wall, then he caught sight of something shiny on the floor. Something that looked familiar. Racing over to the object, he bent down and picked up Julia's watch, and the hair on his neck stood on end.

Then he heard a muffled scream that made his blood turn to ice, and his heart drop with fear. His hand shot to the door handle, but it was locked.

Think. He patted his pockets, an instinctive act, as if he could find a key there to unlock this door. But the hotel key would do nothing. Credit cards never worked except in the movies. He patted his front pocket, touching the outline of the ring. There was no way a ring would open a door. Then he felt the size and shape of the necklace in his other pocket. It was his only chance to get in there before security came, and he had no idea when that would be.

Sometimes you just had to use the tools you had with you.

* * *

Neither one of them could speak. Her mouth was covered by his palm, and he appeared to be shrieking silently from the kicking, sucking in the cries his body must have wanted to emit.

The best part? He couldn't even smack her with his free hand. He was grasping his balls with that hand while wincing and crying soundlessly. So, with his focus on his groin, she tried again to escape, pressing her thumb towards her pinky, aiming to make her hand and wrist as small as could possibly be, narrowing it, turning her hand into itself and tugging loosely, gently.

Her wrist inched past the metal the slightest bit, and her heart tripped with hope. The cuff wasn't too tight. Maybe she *could* slip out of here.

Dominic was still moaning under his breath so she craned her neck behind her, trying to get a visual on the handcuffs to see if she stood a fighting chance of slipping out. An idea flashed through her head. A crazy notion, but sometimes crazy notions took hold of you in desperate circumstances, and with Dominic still nursing his bruised balls, she quietly dipped her free hand into her back pocket, slid off the top of the tin, and scooped out a healthy dollop of lip balm on the pad of her thumb, then began rubbing it on her right wrist.

Lubrication was a splendid thing.

It made objects fit in places they didn't belong. It made engines hum. It made tight rings slip off swollen fingers easily. And right now, it might, just might, give her back the use of two hands. If the handcuffs had been locked any tighter, this would never work. Maybe he'd only wanted to scare her, not to hurt her, so he left a bit of give in the metal. Either way, she'd take those extra millimeters because that sliver of space was her chance for freedom. She was tempted to yank her hand out, but instead she spread the balm around her wrist, and—she'd have to send a thank-you note to her parents if she pulled this off because her hands were on the small side—started to slide it out.

The doorknob rattled.

She flinched involuntarily and glanced at the door. The silver metal was shaking, moving, clattering around. Someone had heard her, or them. She'd be out of here. But wait. What if it was a cohort? She needed to move quickly, free herself, push his stupid hand off her mouth and get the hell out.

The knob shook once more, and Dominic spun around, finally noticing the sound. He dropped his hand from her mouth, and she screamed. Like a heroine in a horror film, she unleashed a blood-curdling cry.

* * *

He'd seen enough movies, had watched the entire library of *MacGyver* three times as a kid. But you didn't live in the movies. You lived in the real world. And just because a TV show hero could pick a lock with the filament from a lightbulb didn't mean he'd be able to pull this off. But he knew the basics—and hell, what man with a brother didn't know how to get in and out of rooms? For Brent and him, locking each other in or out of bedrooms, bathrooms, even the house had been daily pranks, and they'd both mastered the fine art of breaking and entering each other's rooms. You needed to lift the pins from inside the lock. Most doors had five to eight, so the trick was methodically finding each one.

Fortunately, he had a Purple Snow Globe necklace. Though he'd lost his lucky tie, maybe it was luck that the Etsy seller had only had a T-bar clasp because a regular clasp would do jack shit. He needed this one, about the length of a bobby pin. He set to work sliding that into the lock, then listening for the sound of the pins falling. He wiggled it around, prodding, searching for the final pin. When the tension yielded a few seconds later, he knew he was almost home.

It had taken less than a minute.

Off in the casino, he heard movement, the methodical pace of what was sure to be security coming around the corner. He could wait for them or . . .

A scream met his ears. *Julia.* He was all instinct now, grabbing the handle, turning the lock and barging into the room. Adrenaline pumped through his veins, and his fists were clenched. There she was in a chair, yanking her right hand out of handcuffs, and the sight of that made his blood not just boil, but reach volcanic temperature. A slick, sharp-dressed man was pawing at her, trying to cover her mouth with his grimy hand.

No way in all of fucking creation was that hand touching his Julia again. *Ever.*

"Get your hands off my fiancée," he seethed, and everything happened both in slow motion and with blinding speed. In a heartbeat, he grabbed the man's wrist, jerked him away from Julia, and jammed him up against the wall. Clay's hands were gripping the man's collar, twisting it tightly into his neck. He was vaguely aware of Julia rising behind him, moving carefully toward the door.

"Tell her to stay out of my games," he spit back, and Clay answered that impudence by slamming a fist into the man's ribs.

The man doubled over, grabbing his stomach, and moaning loudly. But Clay didn't buy his bullshit, so he served up another fist, then one more for good measure, hoping it would crack a few ribs. A loud crunch echoed through the room. Just then, the first of a fleet of hotel security arrived, led by a pipsqueak woman with blond hair. Clay's breath came fast and he was panting hard.

His eyes surveyed the scene—the crumpled-up man, his own clenched fists, a door broken into courtesy of a necklace in his hands.

This didn't look good for him.

CHAPTER SEVENTEEN

Saturday, 2:22 p.m., Las Vegas

Mindy heaved a sigh, then drummed her short, unpolished nails against her desk.

"I understand everything you've said, but I'm still going to have to report the details of incident to the Las Vegas police department when they arrive in a few minutes, and that includes those two additional punches thrown by Mr. Nichols. The Allegro ownership is trying to run a very tight ship."

Julia steeled herself and gripped Clay's hand tighter, a silent reminder that she was doing the talking right now. She'd told him as much when they came in this room. She knew from the look on Mindy's face when she saw Clay's final two blows that the woman was going to need some convincing, and that she'd need it from *her*—the victim, though she hated thinking of herself in such terms. Besides, she was running on adrenaline now, with perhaps a healthy dose of anger fueling her, too. There was no room in her for fear or worry. She had business to take care of, so she dug in.

"And that tight ship extends to an employee of yours —to the casino's floor manager—working for the mob and accosting a casino guest?" Julia asked, her eyebrow arched.

"And believe you me, that's being addressed," Mindy said, her sweet features now turned intensely serious. "We fully expect Dominic to be arrested, likely on many accounts. He's already been let go since management does not tolerate what he did to you."

"Then why on earth are we even here? He handcuffed me to a chair, locked me in a room, and threatened me because he thought I was playing in games he's rigging for the mob," Julia said, the incredulity thick in her voice. How could they even begin to try to implicate Clay for the two additional punches thrown at the asshole who'd handcuffed her? But anger and annoyance would not win her Mindy's sympathy, so she softened her tone. "He was protecting me."

"I know, and from what I saw you needed it. But even in instances of protection of another person, that protection can't escalate to an inappropriate level of retaliation. Hence my concern over the two additional punches thrown. Look, I have no issues with him breaking into the room. That falls under Good Samaritan law; he heard a cry for help and he heeded the call. But we have to let the police decide if there are any issues of aggravated force."

Julia held up her right wrist, showing the angry red line where she'd tried at first to slide out of the cuffs. "That man handcuffed me in *your* hotel. And I had to get myself out of handcuffs with lip balm in my pocket. Mindy, please. Help a woman out. Clay was looking out for me," she said, keeping her eyes fixed on the woman across from her. Mindy's lips quirked up in a small smile.

"You freed yourself with lip balm?"

"Lubrication is a wonderful thing, isn't it?" Julia said, and she flashed a quick smile too, reminding herself that you won more flies with honey than vinegar. Julia seized the chance to reel her in. "I just think it would be a lot better for all involved, given what happened here and the way in which I was accosted at your casino, if Clay were not brought into this with the police. Do you think you could do me a solid?"

Mindy's smile disappeared. "I wish. I really wish I could do that but we have to let the authorities handle this. It's not a matter of what I think or what I want. I have been contracted by the owners of the Allegro, and their goal is to run things smoothly and deal appropriately with all situations. I am sure, Mr. Nichols, that once you talk to the police and explain what happened when you walked into that room that all will be fine. But I'm going to need to report this. God knows, we have enough trouble we're dealing with at this place right now," she mumbled.

Julia clasped her hands together. She was not above begging. "Please. I just don't understand why that is necessary at all. We'd really like to go and continue on with our weekend," she said. Her heart was still beating at a rabbit's pace. It hadn't come down yet from those moments locked up with Dominic. From the little bit Mindy had told her, and what she'd cobbled together from Dominic's comments, he was running the rigged games for Michael Lawson, and had been assigned to keep tabs on known hustlers. It was a crazy notion that she was *known* for this. But *c'est la vie*. The mob operated underground and this was pure underbelly stuff they were dealing with. "You're Brent's friend. Can't you please just keep Clay out of this?"

Mindy winced, as if this were painful. "I wish I could, but we are really trying hard to root out the pickpocketing that this entire Strip has been facing," she said, and that's when the bell went off.

Ding, *ding*, motherfucking *ding*. Her brain raced back to what she'd witnessed at one-fifteen. To the chip she planned to offer Mindy.

"You have security cameras here, right? Eye in the sky?"

She shrugged, not answering.

"What if I could tell you that it's highly likely the pickpocket was at the pai gow tables at one-fifteen today and seemed to make off with a handful of chips? He was wearing a hoodie and has a rather large nose that I believe is a prosthetic."

Mindy's eyes lit up as if she'd just been handed the keys to the kingdom. "Really?"

"Check it out. See if you see what I saw. And if you do, and I can ID him like I think I can, what would you say to not reporting Clay?"

Mindy chewed away at her lower lip, considering the offer. "Can you wait here for a few minutes? I'll be right back."

She exited, leaving them behind in the open office. Clay turned to her, the first time they were alone since security had rounded them up. Worry was etched in his features. He held tighter to her hand. His touch was comforting, and she sensed he needed reassurance as much as she did. "Are you okay?"

She nodded. "I am now."

"Do you want to go back to New York once we're done? *If* they let us go," he added, narrowing his eyes, huffing through his nostrils.

She squeezed his hand, trying to comfort him, calm him. "They'll let us go."

"Why are you trying to make me feel better?" he said, with a sigh. "You're the one who was hurt. And all you've done is try to avoid me taking the fall."

"I was. But I'm okay now, and I don't want this to get worse. I care too much about you, and your reputation. I thought that morality clause mattered to me. I thought that expanded contract mattered. But you know what?" She reached a hand to him, cupping his cheek. "I don't give a shit what people think about me. I'm a bartender. If I have a rap sheet a mile long, it makes me cooler. But you're a lawyer and you need to be as unimpeachable as you have always been, so I want to make sure you're safe."

He looked at her, such softness in his eyes. "It's my job to keep you safe."

"And you did. You found me."

"I want to get you out of here, Julia. I was only trying to protect you," he said, and his eyes looked terribly sad, as if he felt like it was his fault that he was somehow being deemed culpable.

"You did protect me," she said insistently, grasping his hand tighter for emphasis. "And I'm glad you punched that asshole."

Mindy's footsteps sounded outside the door.

"Hey. Who do you think it is that's pickpocketing?" he whispered.

"Get ready for this," she said with a wicked smile. The first that afternoon. "Tad Herman."

His brown eyes sparkled, and he smiled too. "No fucking way."

"I think it's him, Clay. I really do. He wears a fake nose when he lifts the chips. But it sure looked like him, blond hair, skinny build and all."

"That would explain why he's so hard-core about his morals clause. It's his alibi to cover up his own very bad habits."

She shrugged playfully. "Everyone has a racket in this town," she said as Mindy returned to the office.

Standing in front of them, Mindy held out her hand to shake. "Thank you, Ms. Bell. I believe we'll be able to use that security video from one-fifteen after all. I so value the tip, and I don't recall any additional punches being thrown at all. Everything was done for your protection," Mindy said, and Julia smiled briefly. This was Vegas through and through. A handshake, a deal, a tit for tat. Everyone was on the take in some way—some more above the board than others. But everyone had a price, and she was just damn grateful she'd had the trump card in this round. "If you could just stay and give your statement to the police about what happened with Dominic,

I'd be most grateful. And I'll be sure to let them know about our very Good Samaritan."

* * *

She pressed her forehead to his in the elevator. They were alone, shooting up to the twenty-first floor. "You saved me," she whispered, so much gratitude in her voice. So much need for him.

"*You* saved me," he said, as he threaded his fingers tenderly through her hair, holding her close.

"We rescued each other," she said.

"Yes. We did. Let's always do that." His deep voice was gentle, the one he saved just for her. He brushed his lips against her softly. A rescue kiss. An *only you* kiss. A kiss that said so much about the two of them, how they *fit*.

They were scotch and soda; they were vodka and tonic. They were better together.

CHAPTER EIGHTEEN

Saturday, 3:09 p.m., Las Vegas

Their bags were packed and they were heading through the lobby, eager to catch a cab up the Strip to the Bellagio. He wanted to put the entire last twenty-four hours behind them.

"Are you sure you don't want to get out of here? Leave this town behind us?"

"Do I look like a wuss?"

"Hell no," he said emphatically.

"Then I don't want to go," she said, stopping in her tracks to look him in the eyes. "Look, I don't like what happened, and I didn't enjoy being harassed, but I'm not running out of town with my tail between my legs. Life makes no promises, nor does this city. We could run into trouble anywhere. So if we're living in *The Hangover*, if we're making a pit stop in *Ocean's Eleven*, or even spending a night in *Casino*, then so be it. I'm a gambler and I know there are no guarantees. You wake up every morning and you take your chances. But one thing I am not is a coward. I used to be owned by a mobster a hell of a lot more powerful than Dominic Handcuffs. I'm not going to let some two-bit mob pawn ruin my vacation. This girl is getting her weekend away."

God, she was brazen, and he swore she grew two, three, four feet taller during that speech. He was ready to make a shrine to his badass woman. Instead, he clapped slowly. Several times. "Can I write that down and use it in a screenplay somewhere? Because that was the stuff movie scenes are made of."

"You got a script cooking somewhere you haven't told me about?"

He shook his head. "Nope. No need to, because our life is like the movies right now." He leaned in for a quick kiss, and she grabbed him, tugging him close. He lowered his voice, speaking just for her. "Do you realize I fall more madly in love with you every day?"

"Good. Because maybe that love will make you forget how much trouble I am."

"I love all of you, even your trouble," he whispered, stroking her hair.

She was trembling, and he felt her toughness fade for a moment as she ran a hand through his hair and whispered in his ear, "I really would like you to stay by my side the rest of the time we're here."

"I promise," he said, pulling her in closer, tighter, wanting to make her feel safe now and for all time.

With his arm draped around her protectively, he kept her close as they weaved their way through the afternoon crowds to the doorway, sunshine beckoning from beyond. "A change of pace will do us good," he said. "A fresh start for the rest of the weekend."

"Besides, there's nowhere like the Bellagio to begin our do-over."

As they neared the revolving door, a carrot-topped and freckled young bellman trotted over to them. "Excuse me, Mr. Nichols?"

His chest tightened. What now? "Yes?"

"We had a delivery for you this afternoon. We brought it up to the room but you weren't there, and since you're checking out, my boss wanted to get it to you before you left," the bellman said, thrusting a plastic bag at Clay. The bag was extremely light, as if it were carrying a small scrap of fabric.

He peered inside and there it was—his favorite small scrap of fabric. His lucky purple tie. A slip of paper was wrapped around the tie. He pulled out the paper and opened it.

Clay, I found this on the plane this morning. I know you were looking for it, so I dropped it off at your hotel. Please accept my apologies for the delay. I didn't find the tie on my initial search because it turned out to be wedged between two seats. But after another look, I recovered it for you. The jet is in Vegas now, and I'll be ready for anything you might need, and whenever you want to return to New York.

Clay couldn't contain a grin as he showed the note to Julia. "You know what this means?"

She read it and met his gaze. "It means the tie went missing when we were flying high."

He nodded. "We were distracted. In the best of ways," he said, and they resumed their pace to the taxi stand. As they waited, he slung the tie around his neck, and she knotted it loosely. To think he'd entertained the notion that the pilot had stolen his tie. Instead, their passion for each other had simply knocked the item of clothing out of sight.

Ironic, in a way. Or maybe it was simply apropos for the two of them.

* * *

Dominic couldn't take the smell much longer. He crinkled his nose again, and tried to breathe through his mouth, but he was pretty sure the guy in the corner had just pissed on himself again. The other dude in here smelled like he bathed in a sewer. Gripping the bars tightly, Dominic scanned the concrete hallways, eager for a sign of Michael. He'd called him the second before the cops had tossed him in this cell— tossed being the operative word; they'd practically grabbed him by the belt buckle and heaved him into this pit of pu- trid—and Michael had said he'd be here soon.

He rubbed a hand across his ribs, wincing; they smarted from the beating they'd taken an hour ago.

The sound of scanners and phone calls, along with the grumbled shouts of the temporarily incarcerated, rang in the halls. A cop with a nightstick glared at him as he walked over to the cell. The cop pointed with his chin. "Dominic Stevenson. There's a Michael Lawson here to see you. Come with me."

Dominic's heart ran circles in his chest, taking away the soreness in his stomach. Michael was here, Michael would post bail, Michael would free him. The door opened with a loud groan as the cop unlocked it, then shut it behind him.

See you, suckers, *he wanted to say to his fetid cellmates. But he clamped his mouth shut as the cop escorted him to a small concrete room with a table and two chairs. Michael was seated, his legs crossed, wearing his trademark cowboy boots and a bolo tie around his neck. A big-brimmed hat rested on the table. Dominic reached out a hand, and Michael shook.*

"Man, it is good to see you," Dominic said, and he'd never been so relieved.

"I'm sure it is. I always like seeing me too," Michael said, then shot a toothy smile at Dominic. Michael was like that. Affable; easygoing.

The cop left and they were alone in the room.

"So, you're going to get me out of here?" Dominic asked, hope knotting tightly in his chest.

"Well, let's just talk about things first," Michael said, leaning back in his chair, and tipping it slightly onto the two back legs. "Because I'm not so sure I ever said I wanted you to lock up that lady hustler, rough her up, get caught, and blow your fucking cover," he said, the smile on his face masking the ire in the words.

Dominic nodded, girding himself for getting chewed out. He knew this was coming. He'd messed up, and he'd have to eat crow, but they'd move on and keep on keeping on. "I'm sorry. Things got out of hand. But hey, on the bright side, I kept her out of your games," Dominic said, grasping for the one bit of good news.

Michael nodded several times and chuckled deeply, then pointed at him. "There is that. Oh, you're right. There is that." He stopped laughing, tilted the chair back up, and steepled his hands together. The sharp stare and the erasure of the smile worried Dominic. "But you did more than that, and I only asked you to do one thing: I asked you to keep her and everyone on the list out of my games. I don't want any-one else horning in on my turf, not after the trouble I had with Charlie when I used to work for him in San Francisco.

That cold-hearted bastard accused me of stealing. Something I would never do, but we worked it out and made a deal. And the deal was I'd leave town, and we'd stay out of each other's way. That's all. Plain and simple. And you and Stevie were in touch, you were honoring the deal, and Stevie knew it, and was keeping Charlie apprised."

"We did have a deal. Stevie even called last night and I reminded him, but then she showed up and I had to get rid of her," he said insistently, trying to prove his point. He wanted Michael to see how he'd protected his boss's assets. "I did what you wanted."

Michael made a shushing sound, as if Dominic had been talking too loud in church. "That's what you thought you were doing, and hey, a man's gotta do what a man's gotta do, right?"

Michael stared at him pointedly and Dominic wasn't sure if the other man was asking rhetorically or leading into what he planned to do to him, but either way, he had the sinking feeling Michael wasn't in a forgiving mood. "But I'm pretty sure blowing your motherfucking cover as an inside man was not what I wanted you to do. You're a pit boss at the Allegro. Do you have any idea how valuable it was to me to have you on the inside like that? To know the score? To have access to security cameras and footage and all the intel that I needed to run my games?" Michael shook his head, and sighed deeply. "And now—poof! That's all gone. Because you snapped. When I said find out why she's in town, I meant sit down, have a drink, talk to her like a normal fucking person. Invite her into a game. Find out then if she was working for Charlie. Find out then if I had to be concerned about him encroaching. Liquor her up, ply her with cards and get the four-one-one on Charlie. You should have lured her with candy, not fists. She's a hustler, and you should have invited her to a high-stakes game instead of your fucking office where you cuffed her. You did this three months ago when you tossed a guy out of a game for the wrong reason, and now you've once again gone too far."

Dread snaked through Dominic. He'd botched a previous job for Michael because he was too hot under the collar, and now he'd done it once more. He hung his head and muttered, "I'm sorry."

Michael tsk-tsked. "I'm sorry too. I really enjoyed having someone in my employ working the floor at the Allegro. It was paradise the way you trolled for high-rollers for me. But this, Dominic? This is too far."

The chair legs scraped across the floor as Michael rose, his tall, lanky frame towering over Dominic. "And in case that wasn't clear, I'm not posting your bail. So I guess that means, my inside man is still an inside man." Michael scanned the room, giving it a dirty look. "But now you're on the inside here."

CHAPTER NINETEEN

Saturday, 4:33 p.m., Las Vegas

Over at the Bellagio, they had a view of the fountains from more than twenty floors above, the sprays of water moving to an orchestra, gracefully and in tune.

As soon as the door to the suite shut behind them, she leaned against the wood, feeling like a ragdoll. The weight of the day came crashing down on her in a painful heap of moments—Dominic turning from friend to foe as his fingers dug into her arm; him shoving her into that room; the awful scrape of metal against her wrist as he'd chained her up. She'd been so tough on the outside because she had to be, but inside she'd been scared, and that feeling of helplessness suddenly unleashed itself in her. She felt wobbly and woozy.

Clay wrapped her in his arms. "Are you okay?"

She shook her head against his chest. An errant tear slipped from the corner of her eye, dampening his shirt.

"Hey," he said in a soft, sweet voice, soothing her. "I'm sorry, Julia. I'm so sorry for what happened."

"It's not your fault," she mumbled. Her throat tightened, then another tear slid down his shirt. She wasn't a crier. She wasn't the sobbing type at all. But the tears flowed freely, now that she wasn't keeping her act together while being interrogated by a mobster, or trying to cut a deal to protect the man who'd protected her.

She was safe now from the trouble she seemed to attract like a magnet, and while she didn't want Clay to know how deeply she felt responsible for today, she could no longer hide it. Out of nowhere the waterworks intensified, tears leaping from her eyes to his shirt as she buried her face in his chest, and he held her.

He simply held her. While she was close and warm and snug, he let her cry it out. "I can't imagine how you felt in there. You must have been so scared. And all I could think about was losing you. I can't imagine being without you. You mean everything to me," he said gently into her hair.

"I feel the same about you," she said, wrapping her arms around his waist, clutching at the fabric of his shirt. "And I feel like such a wreck. Like trouble will always find me. What if this never ends? What if I can never shake the mob?"

She felt a gentle hand on her chin as he raised her face so she could look at him. "Then we will deal with every obstacle as it comes. Whatever life throws us, we'll manage."

She breathed out hard, wiping away the remnants of her tears. "But this might never end. I thought I was free when we paid off Charlie, but maybe you can never be free of the mob."

"Maybe you never can."

"I just feel like this is always going to be a thing, Clay. I'm going to keep paying for this over and over. I'm never going to be safe."

"If that's the case, we're in this together, and we'll deal together," he said, threading his fingers through her hair.

Her hair that Dominic had touched.

She recoiled at the memory, like it was a slap.

"You okay?"

She shook her head. "I need to shower. I need to get the afternoon off me," she said and broke the embrace, heading for the spacious bathroom, stripping off her clothes and leaving them in a trail behind her on the earth-toned tiles. The shower was encased in glass, like a fishbowl. She turned on the water, and stood under a steaming-hot stream.

"Want company?"

"Yes."

When he joined her in the bathroom, she was still in that bruised, emotional state as if she'd been scrubbed raw. "Come here," she said, calling him over, needing him with her. She hadn't closed the glass door. Water sprayed onto the floor in small puddles. He stepped closer, and she grabbed his shirt desperately, tugging him close, and planting a searing kiss on his lips. His mouth was soft, familiar and thrilling all at once. In seconds, a rainstorm had visited the front of his white shirt, but he didn't seem to care. Standing outside the shower door, he toed off his black leather shoes, kicked them aside, and then stepped into the shower fully dressed, never once breaking contact with her lips.

He shut the shower door behind them while they kissed, sealing them in their own private misty world of heat. Steam filled the shower as the water washed away the tracks of her wayward tears, the filthy grime of the day. His touch reminded her of all the good in the world. That in spite of her past, in spite of the *kick me* sign she seemed to wear on her back now and then, this man was with her no matter what. The trail of danger that was her baggage didn't matter one lick to him.

As their mouths fused and their bodies collided, she pictured the afternoon slinking away, scooting across the room, and tossing itself out the window. His touch helped erase those moments of fear, and shooed away her doubts, her worries, her guilt over the trouble that tattooed their life. She shed them all, let them fade away for a better moment. A truer moment.

This moment. Right here. Right now. With him. Where she felt safe, and right, and good.

"You," she whispered, as she ran her hands across his soaking shirt, feeling the outline of his hard muscles through the wet fabric. Then his arms, where she traced his biceps, his steely forearms—those weapons that always seemed to come in handy to protect her. "You and me," she added as they sealed their bodies tight, her naked, him clothed, and it didn't matter. She roped her hands around his neck, and refused to stop kissing him. She craved more of him, of his stubbly jaw against her face, his lips devouring hers, his tongue tracing the inside of her lips. She needed his moans and sighs and murmurs as she wiggled closer and closer still, pressing all her nakedness against the sopping wet shirt and pants that couldn't hide how much he wanted her. She rubbed her thigh against him, eliciting a groan.

The sound was sexy, but it was more than that. It was the sound of him wanting all of her. Not just her body, but her heart, her mind, and all the strings she came attached to. The ones that tethered her to a past that sometimes prowled back into their present and gripped them by their throats. He took her strings with no questions asked, just as he took her. She and her troubles were a package deal, and he'd signed up for all of it, undaunted by an ounce of it. "You," she repeated when they came up for air, and somehow it was all she could say. Words were too much. She was overcome, and all she could do was *feel* this love, this future, this unconditional-ness with him.

He roamed her body with his strong hands, mapping her from her shoulders, down to her waist, to her hips. Then, he slid his hands over her butt, cupping her cheeks and somehow bringing her even closer. "You and me," he murmured softly. "You and me. Always."

He reached for the shampoo, squirting some in his hands. He lathered up her hair, massaged her scalp with strong fingers, then leaned her hair under the spray, rinsing out all the suds. He continued to make his way down her body, washing her all over, even her toes as he kneeled before her. Then he kissed his way up her bare, wet legs, caressing her calves with his lips, the back of her knees with his tongue, her thighs with a brush of his mouth. He rose higher, making sure her belly received the same love from his mouth, then her breasts, her neck and her lips once more.

"Thank you," she said, looking into his deep brown eyes. He gazed at her with such love, such tenderness, that she nearly burst from all the feelings that had worked their way inside her, that inhabited her heart, her mind, and her body. All of her belonged to all of him. "Thank you for being with me."

He nuzzled her neck. "No. Thank *you* for being mine."

She helped him take off his soaked clothes, stripping him down to nothing, marveling at his beautiful nudity. "I'm the only one who ever gets to see you like this," she whispered, feeling lucky once more.

"You are."

Ten minutes later, she was dried off, lotioned up and naked, nestled in bed. He joined her, sliding under the covers and wrapping his arm around her waist.

"Clay?" she asked.

"Yes?"

"Would you mind terribly if I just wanted you to hold me right now?"

"I wouldn't mind that one bit," he said, his deep, gravelly voice that she loved wafting over her and settling into her heart where he'd already staked his permanent claim.

"By the way, how did you get into that room?" she asked, curious even as she closed her eyes.

He laughed. "It's kind of a funny story, but I used a Purple Snow Globe."

It was her turn to laugh. "How on earth did you use a Purple Snow Globe?"

"I bought you a necklace with a purple drink on it, and I was going to give it to you today. Brent had it with him. In fact, that was Brent calling me earlier, not a client. He was bringing me the necklace so I could give it to you as a surprise and I happened to have it in my pocket when I heard you scream."

"Wow. You saved me with a Purple Snow Globe," she said, amazement laced in her voice.

"Well, it was the clasp."

"Oh no. Whenever we tell that story, we're saying you picked the lock with a Purple Snow Globe."

"Hey, Julia. Have I ever told you about the time I picked the lock with a Purple Snow Globe to rescue the love of my life?"

"It sounds like a great bedtime story. Tell it to me now."

"Once upon a time . . ."

CHAPTER TWENTY

Saturday, 7:25 p.m., Las Vegas

Dusk settled over the city of sin. The sun drifted far below the spectacular vista of monstrous hotels and massive buildings that dotted the skyline as Clay floated out of dreamland. He stretched and scooted closer to Julia, her naked skin warm against his as neon flickered through the window, the nighttime waking up. The twilight hour danced over the sky, tugging Vegas from the bright, heavy desert sun of the day to the glitter of its neon nights.

He ran a hand over her hip, unable to resist the call of her soft, sweet skin. She murmured in her sleep, an alluring invitation to him. His damn hand had a mind of its own, and he traced his fingertips across the flesh of her stomach, soon drifting below her belly button. She shifted in her sleep, or maybe she was starting to wake up too, as she moved her bottom closer to him. He was spooning her, and his dick was at full attention now, nestled against the soft globes of her ass.

He brushed a kiss on her shoulder, and she shuddered, the soft exhalation sending a wave of desire through his bones, igniting the embers in him. He traveled lower still on her body, his fingertips in hot pursuit. She responded to his moves, parting her legs slightly, making room for his hand. He sought her out in seconds, his fingers slipping between her thighs. His breath hitched at that first intoxicating touch of her. He could feel the hint of her arousal already, her flesh damp against his fingertips.

"Hi," she whispered, in a sleepy voice.

"Hi."

"You looking for this?" she asked, as shifted onto her back and opened her legs for him.

He didn't move for a second. He was flooded with so much desire all at once that it paralyzed his brain and his body, as if all his neurons and synapses had gone into overdrive, momentarily freezing his gears.

He recovered the power of speech and action as he drew his fingers over her sweet pussy, now wet and slick. "Yes," he growled, finally answering her. "I'm looking for you."

"You found me," she said, drawing up her knees and letting them fall open.

He inhaled sharply, the deep breath filling him, spreading heat to the far corners of his body. He dropped a hand to the inside of her thigh, lust jolting through him as he opened her legs more. But it wasn't just lust; it was deep and abiding love. It was the intersection of desire and forever. To be deeply, madly, desperately in love with the woman you wanted to fuck was the greatest rush, the most lasting high.

"You are ready," he said, low and husky, as he moved between her legs, and rubbed his erection through her wetness. She gasped, her eyes floating closed, her lips parting, as he touched her. Her response fueled him—she felt the passion too, she felt the same way he did. There was no other choice, there was no other way but for them both to be cocooned in this cocktail of love and lust. It was only them; they were all there was in the whole world, and she was all he could ever want.

"Please," she whispered, and he didn't have it in him to tease her or taunt her right now. Nor was he going to be rough or tie her up. Right now, he knew—without her saying it—that he needed to make love to her. She needed pure vanilla sex after the day she'd had, so he entered her, savoring the delicious feel of her warmth gripping him.

"So unusual to see you in this position," he whispered, his arms pinned on either side of her as he moved slowly in her.

"Sometimes I just need my man to be on top of me," she said, her eyes looking into his.

"You'll get whatever you need from me," he told her as he thrust into her, and she moaned deeply as she took him in. She wrapped her legs around his hips, opening herself more so he could fill her.

"Come closer," she whispered, looping her arms tighter around his neck, and tugging him near, so his chest was against hers. "I want to be as close to you as I possibly can."

"You are, Julia. You are," he said, as he licked a path along her neck up to her ear, drawing out a heady moan from her as his mouth mapped the column of her neck, then her collarbone, then her shoulder. "I can't stop kissing you."

"Don't stop kissing me," she said, gripping him tighter with her strong thighs as she rocked her hips against him, thrusting back, matching his moves.

He pumped deep into her as bolts of pure pleasure tore through his body, the intensity of being inside her obliterating the world. He rained more kisses down on her skin as he made love to her, wanting, needing—terribly needing—to be as close to her as he possibly could. He needed it for himself, and he needed it for her. He wanted her to feel safe with him always, and to know that what they shared was so very different from how others had touched her body. When he touched her, whether rough or soft, it was always with love, with reverence, and with respect.

"Clay," she whispered, her voice rising in a question, as she pushed herself up on her elbows.

"Yes?"

He rose up on his arms to look at her.

"You called me your fiancée when you came into that room," she said, and it wasn't a question now. It was a statement of pure and utter truth. He hadn't put the ring on her, but she was, for all intents and purposes, his.

"I did, didn't I," he said, pulling her up and shifting their bodies into a new position, so they were both sitting up, and her legs were wrapped around him. He rocked into her, running a hand along her back. "Did you like it when I called you my fiancée?"

"I did. I liked it a lot."

"I feel that way about you," he said, threading his fingers softly through her lush red hair. He wasn't nervous telling her this. Not one bit.

"I feel that way about you," she answered.

"I'm glad," he said, his eyes locked on her gaze as he moved in her. "I want you to be my fiancée, Julia."

"I want that so much," she answered immediately, no hesitation.

Her swiftness emboldened him. He was fearless in their love, certain in how he felt, not just in the moment as he made love to her, but in his heart for all time. "I want you to be my wife."

"I feel like your wife," she said, closing her eyes as he moved in her.

"I feel like I'm making love to you right now as my wife," he said, the words coming out in a heady rush.

"You are. I'm your wife in bed for you."

"I'm going to make love to you like this now, and a year from now, and in ten years, and twenty," he said, raking his fingers through her hair, holding her tight in his hands. Their chests touched, their bodies melded, their thrusts matched as he bared his heart and soul. "I only want you, I always want you; I want you to be my wife, Julia. God, how I want you to be my wife."

"I want you to be my husband," she said, gasping the last word as her body clenched around him.

"I'm your husband, and I'm with you right now as your husband."

"I can feel it, Clay," she cried out as he pulled her closer, never ever able to get enough of this woman. "I can feel you making love to me as my husband," she said in broken breaths.

He felt the build in the base of his spine, his climax starting to annihilate him, to smother his brain in never-ending bliss. "*Julia,*" he rasped out, as pleasure pulsed through him, taking over his mind, his mouth, his words. "Marry me."

"Yes," she cried.

"Marry me," he said again, grasping her tighter in his arms, feeling her heat rush over him.

"Yes."

"Marry me," he said, unable to stop asking as he chased her over the brink, her one word response echoing like music to his ears. "Yes. Yes. Yes."

* * *

What the hell? Was he such a horny ass that he'd proposed to her in the sack? What the fuck had come over him? He wanted to propose to her properly, like a man who had control, who knew how to plan, who knew how to romance a woman, not like a sex-crazed teenager saying whatever the hell he wanted to in the bedroom.

Jesus. He smacked his forehead in the bathroom as he brushed his teeth. He spat out the toothpaste, rinsed his mouth and then gave himself the finger. "You're an ass," he said to his reflection under his breath. He buttoned his shirt and smoothed out his pants, thoroughly disgusted with himself as he ran his hands through his hair to comb it before they went out to dinner.

Great. Dinner. He'd already ruined the surprise factor by not just blurting it out, but telling her over and over. Well, at least the ring itself would be a surprise. He'd tucked it into his computer bag when they switched hotels, and he'd slipped it into his pocket when he'd gotten dressed a few minutes ago. A few minutes after . . . *proposing?* In bed. *Inside* her. He needed to think with his brain, not his dick.

Time for a redo. He was going to have to start this one over. He needed to fix this mess he'd made, and fix it fast.

He opened the door to the bathroom to rejoin her in the suite. He nearly stopped in his tracks when he saw her staring out the window, her back to him, enticingly on display in the black dress he'd bought for her that she'd worn briefly on the plane. He should be used to it by now, the sight of her. But he wasn't and he didn't ever want to grow accustomed to her beauty. He wanted to be blindsided always, like he was now.

She wore black heels and her legs were bare. The silk of the dress hugged her curves, hinting at what lay beneath. She turned around, noticing him.

"Hi."

"Hi."

"You look stunning," he said.

"So do you." She walked over to him and took his hand, threading her fingers through his. "So where are you taking me, handsome?"

"To the best restaurant in Vegas. Blue Ribbon in the Cosmopolitan Hotel just up the street. It's called a *sushi citadel.* The food is said to be as close to heaven as you can get."

She raised an eyebrow and smiled. Sushi was her favorite food. "I'm sold. Take me there."

"It's a ten-minute walk up the street. Or we can take a car."

"I'm a New Yorker now. Let's walk."

She gestured to the door. He was about to head out, but then he stopped, placing his free hand on her arm. He didn't want her to think that was his official proposal, so he'd have to backtrack. He wanted to do right by her, and get down on one knee tonight as he'd planned. "Hey, Julia. I'm sorry for what I said in bed."

She narrowed her eyes, looking confused. "What do you mean?"

He shrugged, trying to make light of it. "I just got a little carried away. That's all."

Tilting her head, she shot him a quizzical stare, as if he no longer made sense to her. He didn't make sense to himself. Maybe the whole day had thrown him off his game. "Carried away?" she said, repeating his words.

"Yeah. That's all. Carried away," he repeated, but as he spoke he had a sinking feeling he might be saying something even stupider than what he'd said when he was inside her.

Why did men have to be such idiots sometimes? But men were, and he was a card-carrying member of that persuasion that often put its foot in its mouth, and there was nothing he could do to yank it out until they reached their destination.

Julia let go of his hand. "Almost forgot my purse," she said crisply, and moved around the bed to grab it from the nightstand. But when she returned to his side, she kept both hands on the purse.

That's where she kept them the whole ride down in the elevator. She barely spoke to him as they walked out of the Bellagio, past the fountains that were lit up against the night, and down the street.

"Are you looking forward to dinner?" he asked, never having felt more awkward in his life. He and Julia didn't talk like this. They didn't make stupid small-talk. They laughed, they had fun, and they talked about what mattered. Was he going to ask her what laundry detergent she preferred next? Discuss the price of bread ten years ago? But hell, he didn't know how to right this ship without spitting out the one thing he wanted to keep secret, so he could barely string together words in any sort of intelligent order.

When they stopped to cross the street, she fidgeted with the clasp on her purse, clicking it open and closed, open and closed. He wanted to say something to make this better.

"The food is supposed to be amazing," he said when the light changed and they crossed the street. The sound of silence was too much. Or maybe it was the sound of having hurt her feelings that sucked.

CHAPTER TWENTY-ONE

Saturday, 8:29 p.m., Las Vegas

She gritted her teeth. The more she focused on keeping her jaw clenched as they walked, the less chance there was that she'd cry. And she was *not* going to shed a tear over this. Let him think she was pissed. That was better than the alternative—him knowing the truth.

The truth hurt like a cruel jester doing a jig on her chest, mocking her.

Because she'd meant every single syllable of her yeses. She'd meant every word she said in bed. Maybe that made her foolish, but she'd thought—she'd actually fucking thought—he'd meant it when he said he wanted her to be his wife. That he felt like her husband. How could he feel any other way? After all they'd been through, and how far they'd come? She *felt* married. She acted married, and so did he. What were all those *always* and *only ones* from him about, then? Had he gotten carried away those times too?

A tear stung the back of her eye, but she sucked it in. She refused to cry twice in a day. Hell, she rarely cried once a week. She was more of a once-a-monther. So she wasn't double dipping in the salty tear-well today. This afternoon had been justifiable. But to cry over a proposal taken back? No way. Not gonna happen.

She should have known better. She wished she could blast out a warning to all the women of the world—don't believe what your man says when he has his dick inside you.

They neared the two high-rise towers of the sleek luxury resort, cars slogging through Saturday night traffic on the Strip alongside them.

He tipped his forehead to the stalled line of vehicles that were puffing out fumes into the night. "Good thing we walked, huh?"

"Yeah," she said through tight lips, her heels clicking against the sidewalk, punctuating every awkward, uncomfortable moment between them.

Once inside the hotel, Julia looked around for signs for the Blue Ribbon. Like every other hotel on the Strip this was mammoth, and the casino threatened to ensnare you. She'd already been ensnared by one today, thank you very much. She'd like to stay away from the *cha-ching* of slots and the *slap-slap-slap* of the cards on the tables.

Fortunately this hotel was all about its ambiance. The lobby screamed *ultramodern* with its cool black and silver design, geometric patterns, and light displays. Mirrored walls, and columns in cubic styles with funky, silhouetted art added to the flare.

"This way," Clay said, pointing to the right.

She walked alongside him, scanning the surroundings —the glitter and too-cool-for-school feel of this place reminded her of the hipster bar she'd run in San Francisco.

The sexy, sleek, sensory feel of this hotel had some strange calming effect on her. Or maybe it was a blotting out. She needed to let go of her self-pity party. So he hadn't meant it when he'd asked her to marry him while they fucked. So what? He'd rescued her from a mobster with a marble loose earlier in the day.

A red neon light flashed at her from around the corner, and when she reached it, she stopped to look. A metal heart hung high on the black wall. In the middle of the heart were the words *I promise to love you* in red neon.

Her damn heart fluttered against her better judgment. The heart really was a wonderful invention, and a thoroughly dumb beast too. She felt him brush his fingers lightly through the ends of her hair. "That's how I feel for you," he said, and rather than be frustrated that he wasn't ready to marry her, she chose to be grateful for the sentiment.

"Me too," she said, looking him in the eyes—albeit briefly—for the first time since they'd left the suite. He reached for her hand, and brought it to his lips, brushing a soft and gentle kiss there. A tingle rushed over her skin from his touch. It scared her sometimes how easily and how much she felt for him.

"I'm famished," she said, needing to shift gears.

"All right, let's get some food in you, woman," he said, and they picked up the pace through the casino on the way to the Blue Ribbon. But before they reached it, a stunning array of lights greeted them.

"Holy shit," she said, her jaw dropping at the purple light that streamed through a gigantic chandelier in the middle of the casino. Only it was more than a chandelier. It was thousands upon thousands of beads of lights draped down from the ceiling, forming an oval curtain of glitter and sparkle that beckoned them.

"That's the Chandelier Bar. Want to get a drink?"

"I'm starving, but oh my God, that just speaks to my bartender's heart like nothing I've seen before. What a gorgeous and ostentatious display," she said, bringing her hand to her chest.

He laughed. "Apt description, and that's only the entrance. Let's go in."

They walked up the steps and into the open bar area, a truly opulent and unique place that would make the

Phantom of the Opera jealous judging from the crystal creation that hung above the bar itself. "It's like those beaded curtains that hang down in dorm rooms. Only, you know, not cheesy and tacky," she said.

"Nope. Not tacky at all. Just a spectacle, like this whole city. Gotta say, places like this are part and parcel of why I love Vegas," he said, when they reached the packed bar. There were only two free seats, and he pulled out one of those stools for her. "This place is all about flash and size and *I'll build a bigger one*. But somehow the city thrives on that. The kind of one ups-manship that brings you things like this—a bar made out of a chandelier."

Soon, a pretty young thing with a sleek blond chignon glided over to them, and asked for their order. Clay gestured to Julia. "Belvedere on the rocks, please."

"And for you?" the woman asked.

"Macallan," he answered.

"Coming up shortly," she said and walked away. Clay turned to face Julia. He cleared his throat, and for a brief moment, she thought she saw the barest of nerves flash in his eyes. "So, I have something for you."

Her heart dared to flutter, like a baby bird trying out its wings. She simultaneously wanted to swat her heart, and encourage it to fly again. "Oh, you do?" she said, giving him a playful look. This was so much better—she'd rather enjoy herself with him than be pissed over what hadn't happened. Yet.

"I do, but I forgot to order ice. One second."

He stood up, and walked to the other end of the bar, finding the blonde bartender. She nodded as he spoke, then he returned to her. "But you know about it already. The gift."

"Oh." Flip-flop. The wings folded in. So much for that flicker of hope.

"The necklace I was telling you about before?" he said insistently, making a rolling gesture with his hand, as if to prompt her memory.

"Right," she said, her mind returning to the story he'd told her before she fell asleep.

He dug into the pocket of his pants, and handed her a small gift, wrapped simply in purple tissue paper. "Fitting color," she said with a smile. She was not going to be ungrateful for this gift, and for all he'd done.

Placing the small package on the metal counter, she untaped the paper. But he stopped her, resting his hand on top of hers. "Wait. I want to say something first. I want you to know how much I have loved this weekend with you, even in spite of everything that went wrong. And it has been my absolute pleasure to shower you with gifts."

Warmth rushed through her body, and she couldn't help herself. She leaned forward and planted a quick kiss on his soft lips, then returned to the gift and unfolded the tissue paper.

There it was. The Purple Snow Globe he'd had made just for her. The clasp on it was twisted, and the sight of the slightly mangled bar made her throat hitch.

"It might still work," he said. "Let me try to put it on you."

She lifted up her hair, and he grinned wickedly at her. "Now, all I want to do is lick and bite that neck when you show it off like that."

"I wouldn't object," she said as the bartender served a pair of mojitos to nearby patrons.

But there was no licking or biting, only the soft slide of his hands as he tried to fasten the necklace. The clasp didn't want to slide in through the hook. Too many bumps and bends in it. He held it closed with his hands. "We'll get it fixed back in New York."

She glanced down at her chest; a silver martini glass with a purple gem on it rested against her skin. A swizzle stick popped out of the glass. "I love it."

"Gorgeous," he said, appreciatively, letting the necklace fall into his hands, and tucking it safely in the tissue paper. "Makes me think of the night we met."

"When you *didn't* order my signature drink," she teased, reminding him of that first night in San Francisco.

"No. But I managed to have one anyway, when I licked it off you," he said, now reaching for her hand. This trip down memory lane had a way of erasing all the frustrations she felt earlier. "And I wanted you to have this as the final gift this weekend, because it only seemed fitting for the last gift to be one that reminds us of how we met."

Last gift.

Then it hit her. This didn't have to be the last gift. It might be the last gift he gave her, but there was no reason she couldn't give him a gift. She didn't have a tangible one with her, but whoever said she couldn't ask him? She wanted to marry him, she wanted to be his wife, and she'd never lived by the rules, not when it came to men and not when it came to life. She was a gambler, a woman who took chances, and even if he said he'd been carried away in bed, so what? She knew his heart and she certainly knew her own. Why the hell did she have to wait for him to officially propose? She started to speak, figuring there was no point planning it out in her head. Just dive in headfirst, and ask the man you love to be with you always.

"Clay," she began, squeezing his fingers tighter in emphasis. "Remember earlier tonight, when—"

He cut her off. "Where are our drinks? This is taking a long time." He held up his hands in frustration.

Her brow creased. "It's busy. It's a Saturday night. I'm sure she'll be here any minute." She took a beat. "Anyway, so—"

He shook his head. "This is ridiculous," he said harshly.

She reached for his arm, trying to settle him. He was never like this. He wasn't an impatient man who bristled at slow service. "It's fine. We'll get our drinks in a few minutes," she said calmly.

"Everyone else is getting their drinks," he said, pointing to the bartender now serving a Manhattan to a man a few seats down.

"Then I'm sure we'll be next," she said, trying to reassure this unexpected ire from him.

He shook his head, and she swore he was about to start blowing steam. His jaw was set hard, and anger flared in his eyes. "I'm just going to do it myself."

He stood up, heading to the other side of the bar. Her jaw dropped. Was he crazy? "Clay," she hissed, forgetting about the proposal. "You can't do that."

"Yes I can," he said as he marched behind the bar and reached for a glass. "Now, I believe it was a Belvedere for you?" he asked, turning around and reaching for the vodka off the mirrored shelf of liquors.

A hot burst of embarrassment splashed down in her body, and red raced across her cheeks. Other patrons were noticing and staring at him as he poured the clear drink into a sturdy tumbler. But the bartender didn't seem to care. "You have to stop," she said sharply. "Just let them do their jobs."

He arched an eyebrow. "I have to stop? But I made you your drink," he said, handing her the glass of vodka. She waved it off.

"Oh right. I forgot your ice," he said, and he dug his hand into his pants pocket, and then dropped something into the glass. She couldn't tell what he was doing from her vantage point, but in seconds the glass was in front of her again, and it took a moment to register what was in-side it. She wasn't sure if she was seeing things or if that was a . . .

She gasped, clapping her hand over her mouth as her eyes widened to saucers.

"Julia, the night we met, you were behind your bar serving me a drink," he said, and there was no more anger in his voice, only some kind of certainty. "And that night became the start of this love. So it only seemed fit-ting to ask you this question here."

She gawked at the glass and she was sure now—there was ice in the drink, all right. A huge, gorgeous, blindingly beautiful, perfectly-cut diamond ring. For the briefest of moments, she felt nothing. Then, like a dam bursting, she felt everything—hope, love, wonder, and unmitigated joy. She managed to tear her eyes away from the ring to look at him, to gaze into his deep brown eyes that were filled with love. "I don't ever want this love to stop," he said. "I want it for all time. Forever. I meant every word I said earlier tonight. Will you do me the great honor of marrying me, Julia?"

She couldn't speak at first. She simply swallowed and nodded, as if that would keep the tears of joy at bay. But it didn't work. In a second, they were sliding down her cheeks. She was sure she'd be a blubbering mess soon. She trembled from head to toe and shook with happiness. "I already gave you my answer. And it's yes. It's only yes. It's always yes," she said, and he reached across the bar to cup her cheeks in his hands. She moved closer, offering her lips for a first kiss as his fiancée. It wasn't their first time kissing, of course, but it felt like a first time. Because it was the first time with this promise. She melted as he kissed her. Her heart took flight. Hell, she might have even launched a fleet of hot air balloons from all the happiness surging through her. Started a parade. Lit up a summer sky with fireworks.

Soon, there was clapping and cheering, and even a few wolf whistles from the line of patrons down the bar. They broke the kiss, and the bartender waved happily. "She was in on it. I arranged it with the bar in advance," he said, then fished inside the glass for the ring. Wiping it quickly with a napkin, he walked around the bar, dropped down to one knee, and asked for her hand. "Marry me," he said, and she could hear the certainty in his voice.

"Yes. A thousand times yes." He slid the ring onto her finger. It sparkled like all the stars in the sky. "It's gorgeous," she said, and that word felt like a cruel understatement to describe this jewel. The ring's beauty was more than the size, more than the sparkle. It was what it represented. Him. Her. *Them.*

He stood and wrapped his arms around her, kissing her hair, her lips, her cheek. Kissing away the tears once more. Only these were good tears. The kind you wanted to shed. Longed to shed. The night they met, she'd never expected anything more than one night; she'd never envisioned that she'd fall so madly and truly in love, that one night would lead to many, would lead to a life together.

"*Julia,*" he whispered, tugging her closer, so she could tuck her face in the crook of his neck.

She kissed him on his neck, then his jaw, and pulled back to look at him. "For the record, and just so you know, I thought you were seriously asking me when we made love earlier. You also need to know, I also seriously meant it when I said yes then. So you got two proposals and two yeses, Mister."

He grinned at her. "I was seriously asking, but then I felt like an ass for asking like that."

"It was actually kind of perfect for us," she whispered.

"And so is this."

"And I also was just about to ask you before you asked me."

He raised an eyebrow. "You were?"

She nodded. "Yep. Right before you walked behind the bar."

"Were you going to get down on one knee too?"

She shrugged. "I hadn't really mapped it out that far. All I knew was I wanted to marry you and I didn't want to wait any longer."

His eyes twinkled, a sparkle in them that seemed to say he had an idea. "You know what? I don't want to wait any longer. What do you say we get married this weekend?"

She couldn't contain the grin, and didn't even try to. "Why I thought you'd never ask."

* * *

Over sushi and more kisses, calls were placed, information was looked up on phones, pictures of the ring were texted, and decisions were made.

When they left the restaurant, he arranged for a limo with the parking attendant. They were driven along the Strip, enjoying it in the way that lovers did: up and down, inside and out, hot, wet, hard, and most of all, full of passion. Deep, true and endless passion.

"This will be one of our last times making love as Julia Bell and Clay Nichols," she whispered to him as they finished another round in the car, the neon lights of Bally's flickering outside, illuminating the night sky.

"I am one hundred percent okay with that," he said. "But maybe we should cap it off with a quickie by the *Welcome to Vegas* sign?"

She winked. "You are my naughty, dirty, delicious man."

"I am, and I always will be," he said, and soon he was taking her by this icon of the city, moving quickly, the risk of getting caught part of the thrill. But they had luck on their side now, and they got away with it scot-free.

CHAPTER TWENTY-TWO

Sunday, 11:49 a.m., Las Vegas

A pile of white tulle, lace, silk, organza and satin littered the couch in the dressing room of the bridal store inside the Caesar's Palace shopping mall. The shop attendant had helpfully corralled all the simplest dresses in Julia's size, but none of them worked. They were all ready-to-wear, designed for a quickie Vegas wedding, but they weren't right for her.

"I can't get married in any of these," Julia said, her lips curving in a frown as she surveyed the heap of cast-aside choices.

"Obviously," McKenna said, rolling her eyes from her perch next to the detritus of wedding gowns. The dresses, though gorgeous, were all simply too much. Too much skirt, too much trim, too much flare. Julia's style had never been showy. Sure, she liked to dress sexy, but she preferred a neat, clean look.

"Why is it obvious?"

"Because you were never meant to be married in a bridal gown, dork," McKenna said with the same sassy confidence she displayed on her fashion blog when she dispensed clothing advice.

McKenna and Chris had landed in town an hour ago. Clay had arranged for the private jet to pick them up in San Francisco and bring them to Vegas for the wedding. Julia didn't want to get married without her best friend— her sister—by her side.

By nine that morning, the bride and groom had already obtained a marriage license. God bless the state of Nevada—no waiting period needed, and the county's marriage bureau stayed open every day, including weekends and holidays. By ten, they'd found a justice of the peace online who was available that afternoon. That wasn't difficult either—in Vegas, they were practically on call, ready to perform ceremonies like doctors delivering babies.

Julia narrowed her eyes. "What does that mean? I'm not classy enough to be a bride?"

McKenna laughed and shook her head. "Hardly. What it means is your style is not typical bride."

"What's my style then?"

Her sister smiled knowingly. "Chic. Maid-of-honor chic."

Julia parked her hands on her hips. "You're the maid-of-honor," she said.

"I know. But I also know fashion, and I know you looked too stunning for words at my wedding, so . . ." McKenna let her voice trail off.

"So . . . so what?" she asked curiously, motioning for her sister to give up the goods. "I love that dress, but I don't have my maid-of-honor dress with me. I didn't know I was going to get married this weekend. And besides, it's black. So what do I do?"

"*You* might not have your maid-of-honor dress, but I do," she said, looking like the cat who ate the canary. Or maybe just a really tasty tuna. McKenna tapped her overnight bag that was still with her.

"But the dress is with me in New York," Julia said, pointing in the general direction of the east coast.

"True. And that's why it's a good thing I know the owner of Cara's Bridal Boutique where we got your dress. Because I called her this morning and asked if she had your maid-of-honor dress . . . *in white*."

Julia's eyes widened with surprise. "Are you serious?"

Her sister unzipped her bag, reached inside and carefully removed a beautiful, simple and alluring dress, the replica of what she'd worn before, but this time in its opposite shade. The shade of her wedding day.

"I knew you wanted to *try* to find something, but I had a feeling you wouldn't like anything you found shopping, so I made a pit stop before we caught the flight. Just in case. Try it on."

Julia slipped the dress over her head, then let the material fall down her body, over her hips, and her legs. It felt familiar and new all at once, from the hug of the silk, to the way it moved like water against her skin, to the smooth, soft feel of the straps on her shoulders. It showed just enough skin to be sexy, and covered enough to be classy.

She twirled once in front of the mirror. "This is the dress."

McKenna launched herself into Julia's arms, hugging her tight. "Let's go get a ring for your man now. You only have one more hour before we have to get you to the church."

Julia scoffed. "Church. Right."

"It's kind of like a church for you, though," she pointed out.

"Yeah," she said. "It kind of is."

* * *

Brent was in charge of backup music, so Clay reminded him one last time. "No funny stuff," he warned, lowering his sunglasses to give his brother a sharp stare as he cued up the song on his phone.

His brother held up his hands as if to say *who, me?*

"Yes, you. Don't think I've forgotten all the stunts you pulled when we were growing up. Besides, if we have the timing right, we don't even need the song."

"No stunts at your wedding. I promise. I'm just glad I got an invite."

Clay clapped him on the back. "Not just an invite. You're the best man," he said, then pulled his brother in for a hug. "I love you, bro."

"Even though you had a crazy weekend in my town?"

"I'm having the *best* weekend ever in *our* town," he said, as they pulled apart. A horn honked loudly from the Strip, not far from them.

His brother wiped a hand across his forehead, and Clay tugged at his own shirt. The sun was high above and was practically shooting balls of fire at them. But it was August in Vegas, so that was that. Besides, a man needed to get married in a suit, no matter the weather, so Clay had on his suit from the flight on Friday, freshly pressed. He wore a crisp white button-down shirt, and his purple tie. He ran a hand down the tie; he might retire it after today. This tie had given him so much already; it might be time to hang it up and thank it for its run. He didn't want to take any more chances with it.

He looked at the time on his wrist. Twelve-forty. Five minutes if they wanted to make the timing work.

"Will the bride be here shortly?"

The question came from the justice of the peace, a smartly-dressed woman with short gray hair and a business-like manner.

"Any second," Clay said, tipping his forehead to the blond man now running across the plaza in front of the Bellagio: his friend, his client, and the husband of Julia's sister—Chris McCormick.

Chris stopped short a few feet away. "They're about to come on down. I had to fix Julia's necklace," he said. "She wanted to wear it today."

"You fixed that clasp?"

Chris shrugged casually. "I can fix pretty much anything," he said, as a crowd of tourists stopped to snap photos. There would be many photos shot here today. They were about to get hitched in front of one of the icons of Las Vegas.

Then Clay's breath caught in his throat when he saw Julia in the distance. Walking down the stone path outside the Bellagio alongside her sister, heading towards the fountains with hundreds of sprays of water forming a sort of elemental backdrop to their wedding. His heart nearly tripped over itself as he took in the sight of her in white, wearing a dress that looked as if it was hand-sewn for her.

He didn't take his eyes off her as she walked closer, the fountains behind them spraying a soft mist that cooled him off. Music played from the fountains, as it often did. "Luck be a Lady." Any second it would shift into the song they'd picked last night to be their wedding song when they found the website that listed the timing and order of the fountain music. Since the wedding party consisted of six people—the justice-of-the-peace, the bride, groom, best man, maid of honor, and Mr. Fix It—they didn't need a special permit. They were just a small group of people stopping in front of one of the top tourist attractions in this town.

As she walked across the plaza, a sprig of lilies in her hands, her sister by her side, the song began: "Fly Me to the Moon" by Frank Sinatra. He and Julia didn't have a song, but this tune fit the bill. *You are all I long for . . . All I worship and adore.* Because that's how they felt for each other.

Soon, she was mere feet away, and he realized he was still wearing sunglasses. Quickly, he grabbed them, and tucked them inside his suit jacket. He wasn't going to be that guy who got married in shades. There. Now she could look in his eyes, just as he could in hers. She stood in front of him, the Purple Snow Globe around her neck, the ring on her finger.

"Fancy meeting you here," she whispered.

"Lucky me."

The justice of the peace cleared her throat as Brent, Chris and McKenna gathered in a small semi-circle beside them, the water behind them. Julia gave the flowers to her sister, and Clay took Julia's hands in his. Her touch sent a charge through him. Holding her hand was still such a thrill, and always would be.

"Dearly beloved, we are gathered here today in this great city of weddings and pairings to join together Clay Nichols and Julia Bell in marriage, which is an institution ordained by the state of Nevada and made honorable by the faithful keeping of good men and women. Marriage is founded upon sincerity, trust, and mutual love," the justice-of-the-peace said, rattling off words she'd surely said thousands of times before. The words both mattered and didn't matter to him. They could be married by a sea captain, a minster, a rabbi, even by someone who snagged his license on the Internet. He didn't care. All that mattered were the *I dos.*

In other words, please be true. In other words, in other words, I love you . . .

The justice-of-the-peace spoke more, but Clay couldn't focus because he was looking in his bride's eyes, the beautiful green eyes that he loved, and that shined back at him with such heart, love and truth. He wanted to remember this moment for the rest of his life—standing under the high heat of the desert sun, without a cloud in the bright blue sky, Frank Sinatra crooning through the water, throngs of tourists passing by, and the love of his life facing him, about to become his for all time. And he was hers. His heart threatened to burst out of his chest with joy.

The justice-of-the-peace turned to him. "Do you, Clay, take Julia to be your lawful wedded wife?"

There had never been an easier question to answer. "I do."

"Will you love, respect and honor her in all your years together?"

Or an easier promise to make. "I will."

She turned to Julia. "Do you, Julia, take Clay to be your lawful wedded husband?"

"I do," she said, keeping her gaze locked on him.

"Will you love, respect and honor him in all your years together?"

"I will."

"The rings, please."

Clay turned to Brent, who handed him the band that they'd picked up that very morning.

He slid a slender, platinum ring onto her ring finger, nestling it close to the diamond that barely matched her beauty.

She placed a ring on his finger. "Now you're mine," she said playfully.

"Always have been, always will be," he said.

"By the power vested in me by the state of Nevada, I now pronounce you husband and wife. You may kiss the bride."

He cupped her face, brushing his fingertips gently down her cheek, wanting to savor the seconds before he kissed her for the first time as her husband. "Hello, Mrs. Nichols," he said, loving the way her new name sounded on his lips.

"Mrs. Nichols would very much like a kiss," she said, and he dropped his mouth to hers, kissing her softly, tenderly as the fountains finished playing their song, and she became his wife outside, under the sun, capping off a weekend that had gone so wrong, but had now turned into the most right thing in the world.

CHAPTER TWENTY-THREE

Sunday, 8:23 p.m., somewhere over the middle of the country

He closed out the email as they flew through the night, en route to New York. "That's done. Grant is taking care of everything."

"Is he?"

"He used to be a sports announcer. He still has contacts at the Giants, so he's calling in a favor," he said, referring to the client he'd wrapped up the deal for on Friday. The very same client who'd said he'd do anything Clay needed. He didn't normally like to call in favors from clients, but he'd learned the hard way that it was better to keep a mobster on your good side. By this time tomorrow, that's where Charlie would be.

Julia rested her head on his shoulder. "I think that's a mighty clever solution you came up with, Mr. Nichols, though I do hope we have no more trouble from mobsters."

He wrapped an arm around her and kissed the top of her head. "That seems a bit crazy to wish for, doesn't it?"

She laughed. "Yeah, it does."

A new email landed in his inbox. This one was from Brent. The subject line was *Check out this post . . .*

He clicked open the email, scanning it quickly. Brent had sent a news story from a local Vegas blog tracking the goings-on in the city.

Allegro Hotel Nabs Pickpocket, Thanks to Intrepid Guests

The newest hotel on the Strip had a very busy weekend. Seems the security team busted the pickpocket ring that had been nicking chips left and right from tables all over town. The culprit? The city's very own Tad Herman was caught on camera and has fessed up. Herman is a former marketing executive at Farrell Spirits, who has a rap sheet for shoplifting back in the day. Seems he never lost his taste for stealing things he doesn't own, and the liquor company let him go. But that's not all, folks! Details are still sketchy, but we're hearing that the hotel also booted a pit boss who was on the take with a certain cowboy in this town. In addition, the Allegro cleaned house, getting rid of a few dealers and some other staffers who were in cahoots. We're told a pair of husband-and-wife amateur detectives played a part in busting both the pickpocket ring and in putting a bully behind bars. Way to go, Mr. And Mrs. Whoever You Are, for helping to clean up Vegas.

They both arched their eyebrows at the same time, and grinned.

"Amateur husband-and-wife detectives, are we now?"

"Not such a bad idea, is it?"

She shook her head. "Not at all. I can just see us jetting all over the world, busting art thieves, solving jewel heists, uncovering all sorts of mysteries."

"Mr. And Mrs. Whoever You Are," he said, trying the title on again for size. "I suppose that could be our next grand adventure. Especially since it seems you might not have to sign that morality clause now that Herman is history."

"So that means I can consort with all sorts of criminal types?" she said as the plane soared through the dark skies.

"Maybe. Or just consort with me," he said, closing the laptop and tucking it under the seat. "Like right now."

"I believe consorting in the friendly skies is a perfect place for our . . . what is this? Fifth time already as husband and wife?"

"We've had a busy, busy afternoon. And let's stay busy this evening. Besides, I have something else in mind for those pearls."

Her eyes sparkled with interest. "What would that be?"

"Let's find out," he said, and silenced any more words with a kiss that felt like magic and movies and so much more.

CHAPTER TWENTY-FOUR

Tuesday, 6:53 p.m., San Francisco

The crack of the bat, the smell of peanuts and popcorn, the whiz of a fastball cutting over home plate—those were Charlie's special pleasures in life. Add in the chance to meet his favorite ballplayer, Buster Posey, and he was a satisfied man.

Clay Nichols impressed him. No one had ever said sorry quite so elegantly or appropriately, finding the perfect gift for him. A special tour of the ballpark before a game. He was really going to have to find a way to convince that man to work for him someday.

For now, he'd kick back and enjoy a baseball game, and tomorrow he'd figure out how to win Mr. Nichols.

* * *

from: cnichols@gmail.com
to: purplesnowglobe@gmail.com
date: August 20, 2:23 PM
subject: The Big Easy . . .

Imagine the crimes we could bust in New Orleans, with all those dark corners, grand old mansions, and voodoo magic.

from: purplesnowglobe@gmail.com
to: cnichols@gmail.com
date: August 20, 2:38 PM
subject: London . . .

I wouldn't mind a trip across the pond for our honeymoon. We could catch thieves trying to steal the Crown Jewels.

from: cnichols@gmail.com
to: purplesnowglobe@gmail.com
date: August 20, 2:51 PM
subject: Paris . . .

Or nab that most-wanted art theft ring in Paris . . . that is, after we kiss, and then some, on a cobblestoned street in Montmartre.

from: purplesnowglobe@gmail.com

to: cnichols@gmail.com

date: August 20, 3:03 PM

subject: Tell me more about this 'then some'

I hear public displays of affection are encouraged in the city of love. That gets my vote.

from: cnichols@gmail.com

to: purplesnowglobe@gmail.com

date: August 20, 3:11 PM

subject: Booking the tickets now.

How about I just show you the 'then some' on our honeymoon?

from: purplesnowglobe@gmail.com

to: cnichols@gmail.com

date: August 20, 3:14 PM

subject: Paris is next for Mr. And Mrs. Whoever You Are . . .

I. Can't. Wait.

THE END

RECIPE FOR THE PURPLE SNOW GLOBE

Julia has always been protective of her drink recipes, but I finally convinced her to share the Purple Snow Globe recipe with me, so I hereby present it to you! Cheers!

The Purple Snow Globe infuses blackberry syrup, ginger, lemon grass and ginger ale for a deliciously sweet drink with that special zing only ginger can bring.

To prepare a classic Purple Snow Globe you will need the following items:

- High quality Blackberry Syrup
- 1-inch cube of peeled fresh ginger
- 2-inch section of Lemon Grass
- 2 oz of Ginger Ale
- Sugar Crystals

- 1 wedge of lime
- 1.5oz of Gin
- Martini Glass, Cocktail Shaker and Strainer

Preparation:

Peel the ginger into a 1-inch cube and smash it lightly. Split a stick of lemon grass down the middle with a knife, and cut it into 2-inch sections. Combine the ginger and one section of lemon grass with 1.5 oz of Gin in the glass portion of a cocktail shaker. Let the flavors mingle for roughly 15 minutes (or longer to infuse more of the flavors into the gin.)

Next, add roughly two tablespoons of blackberry syrup to the mix. Depending on the syrup and your personal taste, you can add more or less to sweeten it. Then, add 2 oz of ginger ale and a squeeze of lime.

Add ice to the cocktail shaker. As you wait for the drink to reach your desired temperature, rub a small section of lime around the rim of the glass and dip the top of the glass into a plate of sugar to create the sugared rim.

Finally, shake the mixture. Aim to break the ice into tiny pieces so the Purple Snow Globe remains chilled.

Enjoy!

Check out my contemporary romance novels!

Caught Up In Us, a New York Times and
USA Today Bestseller! (Kat and Bryan's romance!)

Pretending He's Mine, a Barnes & Noble and
iBooks Bestseller! (Reeve & Sutton's romance)

Trophy Husband, a New York Times and
USA Today Bestseller! (Chris & McKenna's romance)

Playing With Her Heart, a
USA Today bestseller! (Davis and Jill's romance)

Far Too Tempting, an Amazon
romance bestseller! (Matthew and Jane's romance)

My USA Today bestselling
No Regrets series that includes

The Thrill of It
(Meet Harley and Trey)

and its sequel

Every Second With You

and

Burn For Me, a New York Times
and USA Today Bestseller!
(Smith and Jamie's romance!)

Stay tuned for Nights With Him, a standalone novel in the erotic romance Seductive Nights series, starring Michelle Milo and her lover, Jack Sullivan, slated for a fall 2014 release . . .

Jack Sullivan is a sex toy mogul. An extremely eligible bachelor in New York, he's the full package, right down to his full package. Hell, this man could be the model for one of the toys his company, Joy Delivered, peddles. Instead, he's the powerful and successful CEO, and he's got commitment issues a mile-long after the tragic way his relationship with his fiancée ended.

He's looking for a way to erase the pain and that arrives in the form of Michelle Milo. From her pencil skirts to her high heels, she's his perfect fantasy, especially since she has no idea who he is the night they meet at a hotel bar. He doesn't have a clue either that she's the brilliant psychologist his sister has arranged for him to see to help him get over his past. She's simply the stunning woman he takes to bed that night and delivers many Os of joy too.

His touch helps her forget that other man.

When he shows up at her office door the next day, there's no way in hell she's going to treat him after they've slept together. But Jack isn't willing to let go of the first woman he's felt anything for in years so he proposes a deal—share her nights with him for thirty days. At the end of one month of exquisite pleasure, they walk away, having helped each other move on from their haunted pasts.

But soon, all those nights threaten to turn into days as the lines between lust and matters of the heart start to blur. Can two people so terribly afraid of love truly fall head over heels?

* * *

Nights With Him excerpt…

He was no virgin. He was no saint.

But he'd had a quiet year by choice. Guilt had clawed at him, and though he'd had plenty of chances, and plenty of attempted set-ups from women in his office who wanted to introduce him to their sister, their best friend, their cousin, Jack had kept his head down, and his pants zipped. He was a mess in the head, and a fuck-up in the heart, and that had kept him out of the bedroom.

A self-imposed monkhood, his sister had called it.

But hell, he wasn't thinking of his sister right now.

He was thinking how much he'd like that dry spell to end tonight. Maybe even in the next hour. Because this woman was everything he wanted. Sharp, clever, playful and hot as fuck in that blouse and skirt. She had the perfect body for that business woman look she had going on, with the skirt down to her knees that made him think of her in a boardroom, crossing her strong, sexy legs as she sat at the head of the table. She probably ran her own business, and that made her even sexier to him – he was drawn to the kind of confidence that a high-powered woman possessed. And he particularly liked that this high-powered woman had no clue he ran Joy Delivered, because that meant she was actually interested in him, and not the label that sometimes lured others. With the four years he'd spent in the military after college as an army intelligence officer before founding this company, he'd been labelled by the press as the Soldier-Turned-Sex-Toy-Mogul. It wasn't the sort of a title that could be bestowed very often, but it was part and parcel of who he was and though it didn't bother him one bit, he also didn't mind not being that person tonight, along with the baggage attached. He could be himself again. Not a man with a past tethered to him, or a sandwich board slung on his chest.

COMING SOON
AUGUST 2014

The fifth book in the *New York Times* and *USA Today* bestselling *Caught Up in Love* series

Celebrity photographer-in-training Jess Leighton desperately needs to crash the wedding of the year. Snapping just one pic of the A-list Hollywood couple tying the knot will pay her way through school, but with security tighter than the bride-to-be's corset, she'll need more than her camera and smarts—she'll need help from her biggest rival, William Harrigan. Hot, motorcycle-riding Will is the last person Jess trusts, but he's her only ticket in. Good-looking, charming, and British, he's a triple threat. And he's got that sexy accent to boot. Soon, sparks are flying off-screen and in front of the cameras as they devise a plan to sneak into the ceremony. But when Jess's new celebrity client raises the stakes with a photo shoot of the maid-of-honor, she wonders if she's in over her head. Blackmail, Botox, and the worst *The Breakfast Club* remake in the world? It's all in a whirlwind week's work in Hollywood. The audience loves a happy ending, but in a town where everyone's acting and no one's playing on the same team, can Jess find her own happily ever after in time?

* * *

"Harrigan, this isn't the part in the script where the heroine caves and agrees to go out with the guy."

He lifted an eyebrow. "Oh, so I'm the guy in the script? Does that mean I'm the hero?"

"Well, you're either the hero, the villain or the gay best friend."

"Definitely not the gay best friend," he said quickly. "Not that there's anything wrong with that."

"I already have a best friend, and she's a she, so that part isn't being cast for this picture."

"But there are other roles still open? Like, could I be an anti-hero?" he suggested playfully.

Oh, this man was trouble. Too much trouble for my secret little predilection: casting the movies that played out in my head. Naturally, I had to keep going. "Possibly."

"Or what about an accomplice?"

"That's another role for sure. So is nemesis."

"Ooh, I could be a good nemesis. Or maybe even a reformed bad boy?"

I suppressed a smile. He looked like a reformed bad boy. He talked like a good guy. He could be a bad-boy-makes-good. "It's really up to the writers which role you'll play," I said.

"What do the writers think?"

"The writers haven't decided yet."

"So is that a yes to pizza? Because pizza is like sunshine. You can't not like it."

I looked at my watch. I looked at William. I looked at the sky. What were the chances I'd see him again? I wasn't saying yes to a date. I wasn't going to run into him at school. If I hadn't so far, then it wasn't going to happen now. Besides, I'd already proven I was faster on a stakeout than he was, so I'd smoke him as the competition.

He was the ice cream. I was the eater. I didn't need the whole cone.

"Like a date?" I asked, as I furrowed my brow, deliberately wanting to keep him on his toes.

He smiled again. He was imperturbable. "Yes. Like a date."

I stroked my chin, as if considering his request.

I did want a date. Very much so. I knew where it would lead, though. But a kiss? A kiss was just a kiss.

I leaned in, brushed my lips against his, and took him by surprise. He was startled, and didn't respond for about a fraction of a second. Then, he kissed back. A tentative kiss at first, his lips soft as he slanted his mouth against mine. A starter kiss on the boardwalk while the sun fell in the sky, its lingering rays warming me. Then he gently placed a hand on my cheek, exploring my mouth more, running the tip of his tongue across my lips, then deepening the kiss in a way that made me very nearly forget where I was. I shuddered and tingles raced from my stomach to the tips of my fingers, lighting up my insides. The kiss radiated through me, dizzying and delicious, and a promise of so much more.

Stars in Their Eyes releases in late August and is now available to pre-order on iBooks. If you'd like to receive an email when *Stars in Their Eyes* and my other new titles are available, please sign up for my newsletter: bit.ly/1ivx4vT

ACKNOWLEDGMENTS

Thank you to Cynthia and Malinda for brainstorming; to Jen for guiding me through; to Kim and Tanya for their eagle eyes and fabulous tweaks, to my husband Jeff for all the details.

Thank you to Kelly for her wise guidance and savvy planning; to Sarah Hansen for the gorgeous cover; to Ali Smith for her wonderful photography.

Thank you to Lauren McKellar for the rock star editing.

Thank you to Kara for her attention to detail.

Thank you to Jesse for turning my manuscripts into books.

Thank you Cara and Hetty for cheering this story on.

Thank you Kelley for everything you do.

Most of all, thank you to my readers for asking for more.

CONTACT

I love hearing from readers! You can find me on Twitter at LaurenBlakely3, or Facebook at LaurenBlakely Books, or online at LaurenBlakely.com. You can also email me at laurenblakelybooks@gmail.com.

Made in the USA
Lexington, KY
05 August 2014